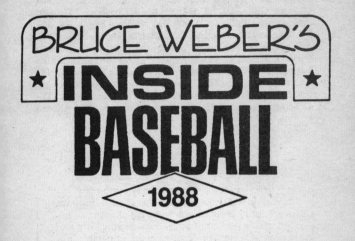

BRUCE WEBER'S
★ INSIDE ★
BASEBALL
1988

SCHOLASTIC INC.
New York Toronto London Auckland Sydney

ISBN 0-590-41716-9

Copyright © 1988 by Scholastic Books, Inc. All rights reserved. Published by Scholastic Inc.

12 11 10 9 8 7 6 5 4 3 2   8 9/8 0 1 2 3/9

Printed in the U.S.A.   01

First Scholastic printing, March 1988

CONTENTS

Front-Office Madness   **1**

Cover Story   **3**

American League All-Pro Team   **5**

National League All-Pro Team   **17**

American League Team Previews   **29**

National League Team Previews   **59**

Statistics 1987   **85**

   American League Batting   **86**

   American League Pitching   **93**

   National League Batting   **96**

   National League Pitching   **103**

Bruce Weber Picks How They'll Finish
   in 1988   **107**

You Pick How They'll Finish
   in 1988   **108**

Baseball's best? Our man is the Yanks' Don
Mattingly, who hits, hits with power, and
fields everything in his neighborhood.

Front-Office Madness

There's something strange going on in baseball. For a hundred years or so, whenever a team went bad, a manager was fired. You couldn't fire all the players, they reasoned. So the manager went — usually to wind up managing another club soon enough, anyway.

This year it's the front-office crew that has served as the scapegoat. Wholesale changes have wiped out the top management of the Indians, Orioles, Reds, Astros, Cubs, and Yankees, among others. Of course, the new guy in Cincy used to run the Yankees and Expos. The new boss in Cleveland (Hank Peters) was formerly the boss in Baltimore. The new boss in New York (Lou Piniella) was the manager last year, while the new manager (Billy Martin) is the same guy who was fired by Yankee owner George Steinbrenner again . . . and again. And so it goes. Interesting, isn't it?

Of course, championships are rarely won in the front office. (And, despite jet-level noise and Homer Hankys, fans don't win championships, either.) They're won on the field with pitching, hitting, defense, running, and just a little bit of luck. So who's going to get lucky in '88?

Your Fearless Forecaster knows, of course. What about the Brewers and Athletics in the American League? How do the Mets and Astros sound in the National League! What

1

do these four teams have in common? They make their living on pitching. Sure, the Molitors and the McGwires, the Strawberrys and the Dorans will do the job at the plate. But it's the arms of Teddy Higuera and Bob Welch, Dwight Gooden and Mike Scott who will get their teammates to the promised land.

Sure, the Cards and Giants, the Twins and Tigers, last year's postseason teams, will be right in the hunt. But the thought of a bratwurst on a cold October night in Milwaukee sounds really good to us. Ummmm. Please pass the mustard.

— Bruce Weber

December 14, 1987

LATE NEWS

After years of limited free-agent movement, things began popping close to press time. Several clubs played key roles in the free-agent derby. Possibly the most important was the signing of Jack Clark by the New York Yankees. His departure robs the Cardinals of most of their limited power. His arrival gives the still-pitching-poor Yanks a powerful lineup.

If we could have stopped the presses, we'd have made Will Clark of San Francisco our NL All-Pro first sacker. That makes Jack Clark our All-Pro DH.

— B.W.

January 11, 1988

MARK McGWIRE

OAKLAND ATHLETICS

If dreams were to come true, Mark McGwire would be trying to make someone's pitching staff this spring. Sometimes dreams get derailed, however, especially when you can hit baseballs over buildings. As a result, Oakland owns the most exciting slugger to come along in years.

In his freshman major-league season, the Pomona, CA, kid blew away every rookie home-run-hitting record. Few hitters, rookie or vet, have smacked more than 30 homers before the All-Star break. McGwire made everyone sit up and take notice with his 33 round-trippers. When the All-Star game was played in his home ballpark, every eye in the place was clearly focused on the 6–5, 225-pounder.

By season's end, big Mark led the AL with 49 homers, finished third in RBIs with 118, led in slugging (.618), and hit .289. No wonder he was the AL Rookie of the Year.

McGwire is the latest in a series of sluggers out of the U. of Southern California. An earlier Trojan, Dave Kingman, also started life as a pitching prospect. But like Kingman, McGwire's bat forced him into the everyday lineup as a position player. Unlike Kingman, McGwire adds a winning personality to his power.

MVP outfielder George Bell is the key as the Blue Jays try to avoid their 1987 fate: a close but second-place finish.

American League ALL-PRO TEAM

First Base
DON MATTINGLY
NEW YORK YANKEES

Have the Don Mattingly Fan Club send us a membership flyer. Have the Yankee Stadium ground crew start preparing for another monument in center field. Don Mattingly is the best player in baseball. One day he will take his place among the all-time Yankee greats.

Serious words indeed, but the man from Evansville, IN, makes it happen on the field. Though he got off to a slow start in '87 (after winning a nearly $2-million-per-year salary battle), Don closed fast. He wound up hitting .327 (fifth in the AL), with 30 homers and 115 RBIs. He also smacked 38 doubles. Among the 30 round-trippers were an all-time record six grand-slammers. Even more amazing, Mattingly had never had a grand-slam before.

Like most players, Mattingly has at least one glaring weakness: He can't run very fast. He has only four stolen bases in his entire career. Of course, how do you exploit that weakness? You don't. Mattingly still plays the prettiest first base in the AL, maybe in the majors. And he can do absolutely everything with a bat in his hands.

After hitting only 37 homers in five minor-league seasons, he's averaging 30 homers in the big-time.

Second Base
LOU WHITAKER
DETROIT TIGERS

Second base may well be the toughest call in selecting the American League All-Pro team. The fans in Seattle and New York may holler, but we'll stick with Lou Whitaker in Detroit. How can you pick Alan Trammell at shortstop without Whitaker at second? After all, they've been together at Tiger Stadium for 10 straight years.

Whitaker doesn't get a charity vote, of course. He won this spot the old-fashioned way — he earned it. Manager Sparky Anderson's valuable leadoff hitter scored a career high 110 runs (third in the league) and slapped 38 doubles (also third). There was some concern when the 30-year-old from New York got off to a .212 start the first month of the '87 season. But he instantly went off on a 25-game tear that helped lift his average to .265.

There was equal concern early about the 5–11, 160-pounder's defense. In the first two months of the season, Whitaker booted the ball 11 times. But as his hitting improved, so did his defense, with only six boots in the last 95 games and only one in his last 43.

If strength up the middle is the key to victory, the Tigers with Whitaker, catcher Matt Nokes, and SS Trammell are set.

Third Base
WADE BOGGS
BOSTON RED SOX

Hear it from Reggie Jackson. "Wade Boggs was born to hit," says the classic slugger, who should know. While most hitters start every season worrying about .300, Wade Boggs, the Boston third sacker, is always asked about .400. Maybe this year.

As usual, Boggs flirted with .400 for a while last year. Only a slow start (.282) as the Sox leadoff man held him back. Once Manager John McNamara put him back in his normal spot, third in the order, Boggs flew. Take June, for example. Wade was actually retired 52 times. But he got hits on 49 other trips to the plate. That's a .485 batting average. As Reggie says, "Born to hit." The AL bat king wound up at .363.

The big change for Boggs was his discovery of power. He slammed 24 homers in '87. That's only three *times* more than his previous best season. In the past, Boggs's critics pointed to a lack of power in Wade's game. No more. Seventy of Boggs's 200 hits were for extra bases, including 40 doubles and six triples. In fact, Boggs finished third in the AL in slugging (.588). That's pretty heady stuff for a singles hitter.

A few years ago, Boggs finished a pregame chicken dinner and went out and got five hits. Now he eats only chicken.

ALAN TRAMMELL
DETROIT TIGERS

Ten years ago, the Detroit Tigers knew they were set at shortstop. They had young, wiry Alan Trammell. A hitter he wasn't. A power hitter he certainly wasn't. But the kid was nice, owned a great glove, and looked like he might improve.

What a scouting report! The glove story was true; the character study was true. But in the last decade, Trammell has found muscle, power, and a tough bat. Maybe he isn't the .343 hitter he was in '87. But the 65 extra-base hits (28 of them homers) were no accident.

"I've become a more patient hitter," says the 30-year-old Trammell. "It wasn't easy, but I knew I had to do it."

Trammell's improvement at the plate was a key to the Tigers' '87 AL East title. With Lance Parrish off to Philadelphia, the Tigers needed a clean-up man. So Manager Sparky Anderson turned to the guy who had only 22 extra-base blows as a rookie. He really delivered. "He's a contact man," says Anderson. "Bring him to the plate with runners on, he'll deliver." Trammell was the Tigers' top RBI guy with 105 last year.

Even after a decade, Trammell and 2B partner Lou Whitaker will keep Detroit strong for years.

Outfield
GEORGE BELL
TORONTO BLUE JAYS

Some of our friends complained last year when we selected George Bell, not teammate Jesse Barfield, for our All-Pro AL outfield. Looking good, they say now. Not that any AL manager wouldn't give his left arm to have Barfield in his lineup. It's just that Bell has quietly stepped to the fore as one of the league's top players.

Except for the final week of the 1987 season, when Bell went one for 29 with no homers, the proud Dominican Republic native enjoyed an MVP year from the opening pitch of the season.

Face it, the six-year veteran carried the Blue Jays when others were failing. He hit .308 (his second straight year over .300), smacked 47 homers (second only to Mark McGwire), led the loop with 134 RBIs, and finished second in slugging (.605) and runs scored (111). Sure that last week was a nightmare. But the first 25 weeks were certainly of MVP caliber.

Bell also plays hurt, which impresses his Toronto teammates. "He gives it everything he has," says Rick Leach. "Try to get him out of the lineup. George won't do it."

The Jays paid George $1.2 million in '87. After his big MVP year, what will he be worth in '88?

Outfield
KIRBY PUCKETT
MINNESOTA TWINS

One of the big questions in Minneapolis this off-season was: "How many r's are in Kirrrrby Puckett?" When the fire-hydrant-shaped Twin center fielder is announced on the Homerdome P.A. system, it's always Kirrrrby. That's just fine with the chunky 5–8, 210-pounder who does amazing things on the field and at the plate.

No doubt Puckett is the spark plug in Manager Tom Kelly's machine. It took the play-offs and World Series for the rest of the country to develop an appreciation for the 26-year-old star. But the Homer Hanky wavers in Minny have known that their favorite No. 3 hitter, who also steals homers by using his great speed and leaping ability in the OF, is the main man.

Last season was typical for the Chicago native. He hit .332 to rank fourth in the AL. He also smacked 28 homers, banged out 32 doubles, and swiped a dozen bases. His 207 base hits tied Kaycee's Kevin Seitzer for the league lead, and he won his second Rawlings Gold Glove.

But Kirby's (make that Kirrrrby's) major attraction is his explosiveness. He's the guy who makes things happen for the Twins. Excitement is his middle name. Or maybe that should be "Exciiiiiitement!"

Outfield
DWIGHT EVANS
BOSTON RED SOX

At an age when most American Leaguers (and probably some National Leaguers) dream of spending their declining years as designated hitters, Dwight Evans of the Boston Red Sox is intent on remaining the AL's best right fielder.

An entire generation of New Englanders has grown up watching Dewey Evans patrolling Fenway Park's outfield. He is both the oldest Red Sox in age and in years of service for Boston. He has been out there in right practically everyday since 1972. And if his 1987 performance is any indication, he may be there a few more years.

Evans smacked the ball at a .305 clip; tied for third in the AL in homers with 34; tied for seventh in doubles with 37; and knocked in 123 runs, second only to George Bell's 134. Not bad for a 36-year-old coming off double knee surgery.

The secret of Evans' success? Hard work and total dedication. It's a lesson Dwight learned from another old Red Sox, Carl Yastrzemski. "Yaz didn't have the world's greatest talent," says Evans, "but had this great desire to be No. 1. So do I." With a great batting eye, outstanding power, and a rifle for a throwing arm, Dwight Evans may well be No. 1 — for years to come.

Catcher
MATT NOKES
DETROIT TIGERS

This vote for Matt Nokes as the American League's All-Pro catcher might be a case of too much too soon. Maybe we're a year or so early. But eventually, Nokes will be the AL's best backstop or, at worst, its best designated hitter.

When long-time Tiger catching star Lance Parrish decided to cast his lot with the Phillies, Detroit turned its eyes toward Dwight Lowry, with Mike Heath providing depth. Few thought about Nokes, who had hit .285 at Nashville before playing seven games for the 1986 Tigers. Earlier he had played 19 games for the Giants, coming to Detroit in a six-player deal.

But when they took the wraps off the '87 season, the 6-1, 185-pounder from San Diego uncovered a potent bat that made everyone in the AL sit up straight. By the All-Star break, Nokes had swatted 20 homers and knocked in 51 runs. Forget Lance Parrish. Despite an 18-for-102 slump, he went on a tear (28 for 67) when the pennant was on the line in September. Nokes, the first Tiger rookie in 50 years to smack 30-or-more homers, wound up with 32 round-trippers and 87 RBIs, hitting .289.

At age 24, Nokes still has to work on his defense. But his future is brilliant.

Pitcher
ROGER CLEMENS
BOSTON RED SOX

Forget the Cy Young jinx! Anyone who believed that winning the Cy Young Award set the victor on a downward track need only check Roger Clemens' 1987 performance. He's the AL's best, winning the Cy Young Award for the second straight year.

A preseason holdout promised big trouble for the Boston righty. Without spring training, he got off to a 4–6 start. "We told you so," crowed the jinx crowd. They didn't know Roger. Pitching for a so-so Boston club, Clemens won 16 of his last 19 starts, won his 20th on the last day of the season, and became the AL's first back-to-back 20-game winner (he was 24–4 in '86) since Tommy John of the Yankees in '79 and '80.

There were other statistical crowns for Roger last year, too. He led the majors in shutouts with seven and in complete games with 18. He was the AL's busiest pitcher (281⅔ innings), finishing second in strikeouts (256) and third in ERA (2.97).

People tended to forget Clemens as the Sox slumped from the 1986 AL championship to a 78–84 record in 1987. That disappointed Clemens but did not distract him. "A lot of folks didn't think I could win 20 again last year," says Clemens. "They were wrong. Now I'll have to do it again in '88."

14

Pitcher
JIMMY KEY
TORONTO BLUE JAYS

On opening day Toronto Blue Jay left-hander Jimmy Key knew '87 would be a good year. He gave up only two runs and three hits in six innings as Toronto beat Cleveland 7–3. The year before, he lost his first three games, didn't win until mid-May, and had an ERA of 13.27. What a difference a year makes!

The stars must have been in all the right places throughout the season. Key wound up leading the AL with a 2.76 ERA, led his club with 17 wins, and helped the Jays take the team ERA title (3.74). Were it not for the last-week collapse that cost Toronto the Eastern Division title, the world would have learned about the young lefty.

Consistency is the key to Key. He hardly ever pitches a bad game. When the Jays give him just a little support he wins. Remember the Jays' last-game 1–0 loss? The losing pitcher was Jimmy Key. A lawsuit for lack of support would certainly be in line. (It's an old story. The Jays were shut out in three of Key's 1986 starts, too.)

The ability to get ahead of hitters has helped the 27-year-old Key become one of the AL's best. "I'm not the kind of pitcher who can work behind in the count," says Key. "If I can stay ahead, I can win."

15

Something about Chicago's day games and real grass did wonders for the Cubs' MVP outfielder Andre Dawson, NL homer king.

16

National League
ALL-PRO TEAM

First Base
JACK
CLARK
ST. LOUIS CARDINALS

Minnesota fans, would you please put down your Homer Hankies for a moment. There, that's better. Congratulations, folks. Your Twins won it fair and square. But if you think that the absence of Jack Clark from the Cardinal lineup didn't help your guys, you're nuts.

NL managers absolutely hate seeing Clark step to the plate. Chances are that one or more of his teammates — Vince Coleman, Ozzie Smith, Tommy Herr — will be on base, ready to come around to score. And as often as not, big Jack will deliver. Despite missing almost the entire final month of the regular season (plus the play-offs and Series), Jack set career highs with 35 homers and 106 runs batted in.

Opponents' fear helped make Clark the king of the walkers (he received 136 free passes in '87). He also led the loop in slugging (.597) and on-base (.459) percentage.

A good, if not great, glove man at first, Clark will be aiming for another MVP-type year in '88. "I thought I had a real chance last year before the injury," says Clark. "That ruined it. But I'm not worried. I'll have other chances."

A full season as good as his ⅚ season in '87 could do it.

Second Base
JUAN SAMUEL
PHILADELPHIA PHILLIES

The press in Philadelphia is running out of adjectives to describe All-Pro second sacker Juan Samuel. After all, how many times can you hang the same labels — *dynamic, exciting,* and all the rest? (New nominations should be sent to the Phils.)

Mike Schmidt may be the guy who gets the job done in Philly. But Samuel is the fellow who makes things happen. In each of his four major-league seasons, he has reached double figures (10 or more) in doubles, triples, home runs, and stolen bases. The 1987 numbers included 37 two-baggers (fourth in the NL), 15 three-base hits (tops in the league), 28 homers, and 35 steals. No National Leaguer ever accomplished that in his first four seasons — until Samuel.

Juan's major shortcoming is that he simply strikes out too much. Before last season, it looked like he was cutting down on his whiffs. But in '87 he fanned 162 times, an average of just about once a game for Samuel, who played in 162 games. That's the only thing standing between Juan and superstardom. Though the Phils finished in the NL East's second division in '87, Samuel is the player who could help elevate them back to the top.

Third Base
TIM WALLACH
MONTREAL EXPOS

Manager Buck Rodgers was named Manager of the Year. Left fielder Tim Raines helped rally the club once he finally signed his '87 contract. But it was third sacker Tim Wallach who really keyed the near-miracle in Montreal.

Wallach, who has never gotten the respect he deserves among NL third basemen because the Phillies have a guy named Schmidt, had his best year ever in '87, at-bat and in the field.

Three tough injuries — broken toe, sprained wrist, fractured ankle — destroyed Wallach in '86. There were doubts. But Tim's '87 performance erased them — forever. His 123 RBIs were a career high and second only to ex-teammate Andre Dawson. He smacked 26 homers and hit .298 while leading the league in doubles with 42.

Despite his performance, Tim is ready to pass the credit around. Replacing Hubie Brooks as the clean-up hitter was the key, Wallach says. "Batting in front of Hubie and Andres Galarraga gave me lots more good pitches to hit."

To Manager Rodgers, however, the key is Wallach's attitude. "He's a team man all the way," says Buck. "No one wants to win more than Wallach."

Shortstop
OZZIE SMITH
ST. LOUIS CARDINALS

TV announcers tend to overdo things. They are given to words like *greatest*, *best*, *most wonderful*. You get the idea.

Throughout the major-league play-offs and World Series, the folks who talk on the tube described Cardinal shortstop Ozzie Smith as "the greatest ever." He may be. We doubt it. Ever is a long time. But the Wizard of St. Louis is the best there is today and over recent history, too.

Ozzie is Mr. Consistency for Whitey Herzog's NL champions. Defensively, he's in a class by himself. He makes difficult plays that no one else makes and makes everyone else's difficult plays look easy. Add Ozzie's super-accurate arm to the glove and you have the king of today's shortstops.

But Ozzie also led the Redbirds in batting (.303), had 182 hits (third in the NL), smacked 40 doubles (tied for second), and stole 43 bases. He also has the tough task of hitting behind Vincent Coleman, whose baserunning activities complicate Ozzie's job at the plate.

The key word for Ozzie, though, is *leader*. The Cards withstood numerous problems on their way to the NL East victory over New York and Montreal. Ozzie, as always, was the glue that held it all together.

Outfield
ANDRE DAWSON
CHICAGO CUBS

Talk about perfect marriages: Andre Dawson and Wrigley Field. When Andre decided he no longer wanted to play in Montreal a couple of winters ago, he set dead aim on Chicago. He got far less money than he might have somewhere else — including Montreal. But Dawson had his mind made up.

"I see the ball better during the day," says Dawson. "I'm looser and more relaxed. I like seeing the sun." He gets to see the big yellow ball for all of the Cubs' 81 home games in the friendly confines of Wrigley.

But what accounts for Andre's MVP year: 49 homers and 137 RBIs (both league-leading figures and the NL's best in 10 years)? "I'm stronger now," says Dawson. "There are a lot of balls that I hit that I *know* are going out of the park. I've grown up — physically and mentally."

Amazingly, Dawson's home-run stats included two long dry spells. Andre didn't hit a home run between June 7 and July 5 (92 at-bats) or between August 30 and September 14 (46 at-bats). But overall, Andre has matured at the plate. "I've cut down on my swing with runners on base. That produced a lot more RBIs. Now I hope I can keep it up and help the Cubs move up."

22

Outfield
TIM RAINES
MONTREAL EXPOS

Tim Raines causes enormous problems for Expo Manager-of-the-Year Buck Rodgers. Should Raines bat first? Should he bat third? Deep problems indeed.

No matter where he bats, Tim Raines is a threat. The NL's leading hitter in '86 (.334), Tim "slumped" to only .330 (third in the NL) last year. The league's best leadoff hitter batted in the third spot most of the season, thanks in part to an injury to shortstop Hubie Brooks. But Rodgers concedes that Raines is the best leadoff man in the game and is likely to have him back there this season.

"Tim's a great line-drive hitter," says Rodgers. "He can do so many things so well. But he probably gets better pitches to hit when he's in the top spot."

Tim missed the first month of the '87 season. He went the free-agent route, trying for more money. No one bit, however, and Tim re-signed with Montreal. In his first game, he smacked five hits and won the game with a 10th-inning grand-slam homer. So much for the value of spring training!

Raines still wound up leading the NL in runs scored (123), stole 50 bases, smacked 34 doubles and 18 homers, and led the Expos' "just short" effort at the NL East title.

23

Outfield
TONY GWYNN
SAN DIEGO PADRES

The good news for National League managers is that Tony Gwynn predicts his batting average will go down in '88. The bad news is that Gwynn intends to get stronger and hit with more power. What a combination!

Most experts will concede that Boston's Wade Boggs and Gwynn are the best pure hitters in the game today. Still, Tony is stung by the critics. They say he's a one-way hitter. "All he can do is hit singles," they say. (Not terrible, we say.) But Tony believes he can be even more valuable and help the Padres more if he increases his power. An interesting problem.

True, 162 of Tony's major-league-leading 218 hits last year were singles. True, only seven of those hits were home runs. But it's hard to argue with Tony's success. He had 34 more hits (count 'em — 34) than any other National Leaguer. And his 36 doubles and 13 triples put him right near the top of the league. (He also stole 56 bases, which placed him a distant second to St. Louis' Vincent Coleman.)

A two-time Gold Glove outfielder, Gwynn is still the top choice to win the NL bat title in '88 — unless he really tries to win the home-run title!

Catcher
BENITO
SANTIAGO
SAN DIEGO PADRES

Benito Santiago doesn't look like a catcher. The Padres' backstop has skinny arms, skinny legs, a skinny body. But the arm is powerful, the body strong enough, and the spirit more than willing.

The Padres knew they had something special in Santiago when they traded Terry Kennedy, a veteran pro, to the Orioles before Benito's rookie year. Everyone else thought San Diego was nuts. Wrong! Santiago had everything they were looking for on defense and his arm scares National League base runners. Then, when he hit in 34 straight games at the end of the '87 season, he sold everyone. Since 1900 only two National Leaguers (Pete Rose and Tommy Holmes) have had longer streaks.

A one-time Little League shortstop from Puerto Rico, Santiago was a key man as the Padres rallied from a horrible 12–42 start to become one of the West's hottest teams by October. He's aggressive at-bat. He walked only 16 times in 572 trips to the plate.

Still, thanks to his late-season tear, Santiago hit .300 (.346 during the streak), with 18 homers and 79 RBIs. He even had 21 stolen bases. The NL Rookie of the Year, he should be the Padres' catcher for a decade.

25

Pitcher
DWIGHT GOODEN
NEW YORK METS

The National League's best pitcher? There's no question. If he stays out of trouble (and we think he will), it's the Mets' righty, Dwight Gooden.

The 6-3, 198-pounder finally got his act together (and his first big-league start) on June 5 last season, and he immediately showed why opponents look for excuses not to play when he's on the mound. After a month in a rehab center and another in the Mets' minor-league system, New York's main guy won his first start (5–1), took five of his first six decisions (losing only when the team was shut out), and led the Mets back into the NL race (they were out of it at the All-Star break).

Met fans insist that New York would have beaten St. Louis had Gooden's comeback begun sooner than June 5. We'll never know. But if Gooden is available from opening day in '88, the Mets' chances for another World Series visit improve tremendously. Remember, only four NL pitchers won more games than Dwight.

The key is mental preparation. If Gooden has his head on straight, there's usually no contest. The master of the blazing fastball and sharp-breaking curve can win every time he goes to the mound.

Pitcher
RICK SUTCLIFFE
CHICAGO CUBS

Why did the Cubs and president/general manager Dallas Green decide to part company last winter? Possibly because the Cubs finished last in the NL East despite fielding the league's top hitter (Andre Dawson) and, arguably, its best pitcher (Rick Sutcliffe).

Certainly, Dawson's case is stronger. Fans of Dwight Gooden, Rick Reuschel, Orel Hershiser, and Steve Bedrosian will argue with any No. 1 award for Sutcliffe. But it's hard to imagine where the Cubs would have been without the lanky right-hander who won nearly one quarter of all the Cubs' victories.

The NL's top winner with 18 (the Cubs had 76 wins), Sutcliffe would have traded all of his stats for a better finish by the ball club. "I'm sure that goes for Andre [Dawson], too," says Sutcliffe. "It's tough to think of your numbers when your team is last."

Barring some major changes in Chicago, another last-place finish is possible. Still, Sutcliffe will be ready for another top season. The 1984 Cy Young Award winner (16–1) closed last year on a high note. In mid-September, he won three straight complete games. The Cubs went 0–7 in the games he did not pitch.

If the A's Dave Stewart can put together another year like his 20–13 1987 season, folks will stop calling him "Dave Who?"

American League TEAM PREVIEWS

AL East
MILWAUKEE BREWERS
1987 Finish: Third
1988 Prediction: First

Paul Molitor   **Teddy Higuera**

The '87 Brewers got off to a rolling start, slumped, then finished strong to become the surprise team of the AL East. No one would have believed that the Brewers would enjoy the fifth-best record in the majors last year. But they did — and the future looks even better.

Young manager Tom Trebelhorn, who doubles as a substitute teacher in Portland, OR, during the off-season, looks for improved starting pitching and improved health for his team starting the new year.

There's good balance on offense. 1B Greg Brock, once a Dodger disappointment, hit .299, with 85 RBIs a year ago. 2B Juan Castillo needs to improve his stickwork (.224), as does SS Dale Sveum (.252); but Sveum's 95 RBIs make him a most valuable Brewer.

The outfield is in excellent shape, with veteran CF (and former infielder) Robin Yount (.312 and 103 RBIs) the leader. Look for RF Glenn Braggs (.249) and fleet LF Mike Felder (.266, but .309 right-handed) to get the job done. There will, of course, be a spot for DH Paul Molitor, the AL's second-leading hitter (.353), whose 39-game hitting streak excited baseball fans everywhere last summer. Rob Deer will have to cut down on his strikeouts (an AL record 186 last year). B.J. Surhoff (.299) could well be the AL catcher of the future.

Pitchers Juan Nieves (14–8, including an early no-hitter) and Teddy Higuera (18–10) were both AL Players of the Week in '87 and figure to lead the mound staff. More depth is required. The bullpen is in the able hands of Dan Plesac (5–4, 23 saves) and Chuck Crim (6–8, 12 saves).

Outfielder Lavelle Freeman, whose .395 average (at El Paso) was pro baseball's highest in '87, is a top future prospect.

STAT LEADERS — 1987

BATTING

Average: Molitor, .353
Runs: Molitor, 114*
Hits: Yount, 198
Doubles: Molitor, 41*
Triples: Yount, 9
Home Runs: Deer, 28
RBIs: Yount, 103
Stolen Bases: Molitor, 45

PITCHING

Wins: Higuera, 18
Losses: Wegman, 11
Complete Games:
 Higuera, 14
Shutouts: Higuera, 3
Saves: Plesac, 23
Walks: Nieves, 100
Strikeouts: Higuera, 240

*Led league.

AL East
TORONTO BLUE JAYS
1987 Finish: Second
1988 Prediction: Second

Lloyd Moseby   **Tony Fernandez**

Some Blue Jay fans still wake up in a cold sweat. The nightmare of the last week of the '87 season continues, though the Jays are advised to forget it, starting '88.

There's no reason why Manager Jimy Williams and his guys can't bring an AL East flag to Ontario in '88. The outfield — MVP George Bell, Lloyd Moseby, and Rawlings Gold Glover Jesse Barfield — is baseball's best. And Bell (.308, 47 homers) may be the game's top outfielder, despite a final-week swoon.

In the infield, the key is the healthy return of star SS Tony Fernandez (.322) who missed the last week with a busted elbow after getting by on a gimpy knee. 1B Willie Upshaw knocked in only 58 runs last year, which could spell the end of his reign as the

Jay first sacker. Look for Manager Williams to platoon Fred McGriff (20 homers in 107 games as a rookie) and Cecil Fielder (.269) at that spot. That may well turn Rance Mulliniks (.310) and Juan Beniquez (.261) into the Jay DH platoon. Nelson Liriano (.241) impressed late last year, and Williams may find a spot for him. Third base remains a question mark. A healthy Ernie Whitt (.269) solidifies the catching picture, where Greg Meyers will press for a job.

The AL's ERA leader (2.72) and Cy Young award runner-up, Jimmy Key, will be the key to the Jay mound staff. His contract was instantly renewed by the Toronto management. A healthy Dave Stieb (13–9) will help, though with Tom Henke (9–6, 2.49, 34 saves), the starters aren't under pressure to go nine. Jim Clancy (15–11) and Mark Eichhorn (10–6, 3.17) are also vital to Williams' pitching plans. Duane Ward, Todd Stottlemyre, and David Wells are ready to help in the major leagues.

STAT LEADERS — 1987

BATTING
Average: Fernandez, .322
Runs: Bell, 111
Hits: Bell, 188
Doubles: Bell, 32
Triples: Fernandez, 8
Home Runs: Bell, 47
RBIs: Bell, 134*
Stolen Bases: Moseby, 39

PITCHING
Wins: Key, 17
Losses: Clancy, 11
Complete Games:
   Key, 8
Shutouts: Three with 1
Saves: Henke, 34*
Walks: Stieb, 87
Strikeouts: Clancy, 180

*Led league.

AL East
DETROIT TIGERS
1987 Finish: First
1988 Prediction: Third

Jack Morris   **Kirk Gibson**

Blessed with a veteran roster and solid starting pitching, the Detroit Tigers figure to make Manager Sparky Anderson look brilliant again in '88. Though they came up a little short against the Twins, the '87 Tigers made for exciting times in the Motor City. There will be more this season.

The off-season questions centered around pitcher Jack Morris, third base, and right field. If free-agent Morris (18–11, 3.38) is back, the Tigers are set. Walt Terrell (17–10) and Frank Tanana (15–10) complete a solid starting trio. There are some holes in the bullpen staff, where Mike Henneman (11–3, 2.98, seven saves) is the key. If Doyle Alexander, who went 9–0 with a 1.53 ERA in his 11 starts in Detroit, pitches back to his '87 form, the bullpen may not be as important.

Darrell Evans (.257), whose age will match his uniform number (41) in May, is back at first base after a 34-homer season. The middle defense is in the capable hands of All-Pros 2B Lou Whitaker (.265) and SS and MVP runner-up Alan Trammell (.343). The pair, who have played together for 10 straight seasons, could have another five years. Third base is a trouble spot, though rookie Doug Strange looks like he's ready to step in soon.

The outfield is two-thirds set. LF Kirk Gibson missed 34 games in '87, yet hit .277 with 24 homers and 79 RBIs. Chet Lemon will be back in center, following his .277 and 20-homer campaign. The outfield question revolves around right field where Pat Sheridan (.259) will be hard-pressed by Scott Lusader, who impressed in September with his .319 bat mark and overall sterling play. C Matt Nokes is the AL All-Pro after his 32-homer, 87-RBI debut. Mike Heath is solid, too.

STAT LEADERS — 1987

BATTING
Average: Trammell, .343
Runs: Whitaker, 110
Hits: Trammell, 205
Doubles: Whitaker, 38
Triples: Whitaker, 6
Home Runs: Evans, 34
RBIs: Trammell, 105
Stolen Bases: Gibson, 26

PITCHING
Wins: Morris, 18
Losses: Morris, 11
Complete Games:
    Morris, 13
Shutouts:
    Alexander, Tanana, 3
Saves: King, 9
Walks: Terrell, 94
Strikeouts: Morris, 208

AL East
NEW YORK YANKEES
1987 Finish: Fourth
1988 Prediction: Fourth

Rick Rhoden   **Willie Randolph**

We don't understand George Steinbrenner. They say he's a great businessman. But if he runs his other businesses as he runs the Yankees, we have doubts. Unhappy with Lou Piniella as manager ("he doesn't have enough experience"), he makes Lou the general manager (no experience at all). Then he picks Billy Martin (fired four times before) as the field manager. That will last at least into May. Don't ask about June!

Sweet Lou's first two deals brought the Yankees catcher Don Slaught and pitcher Rich Dotson, neither of whom are the answers to key Yankee questions. Will George and Lou continue to empty the Yank farm system for questionable talent?

There's nothing questionable about some of the present Yanks. 1B Don Mattingly, who someday will be baseball's highest-paid player, is baseball's best player. In an "off" season last year, he hit .327, hit 30 homers (including a record six grand slams), and knocked in 115 runs. 2B Willie Randolph remains a solid citizen (.305, fine fielding, great leadership skills). The arrival of ex-Met Rafael Santana ends the shortstop derby. Powerful Pags (Mike Pagliarulo) should be at third. Though Rickey Henderson (.291 in only 95 games) isn't a Billy Martin fan, he'll likely be back (in left) to key the outfield with RF Dave Winfield (27 homers, 97 RBIs). But battles will continue in left and behind the plate. The Yanks used 48 players last season!

With some prayers from George, Dotson will join a starting rotation with lots of holes, led by Rick Rhoden (16–10), Ron Guidry (5–8 and coming off shoulder surgery), ageless Tommy John (13–6), and Bill Gullickson. Charles Hudson (11–7) should be on again, with Dave Righetti (31 saves) the king of the bullpen crew.

STAT LEADERS — 1987

BATTING	PITCHING
Average: Mattingly, .327	Wins: Rhoden, 16
Runs: Randolph, 96	Losses: Rhoden, 10
Hits: Mattingly, 186	Complete Games:
Doubles: Mattingly, 38	Hudson, 6
Triples: Henderson, Pagliarulo, 3	Shutouts: Hudson, 2
Home Runs: Pagliarulo, 32	Saves: Righetti, 31
RBIs: Mattingly, 115	Walks: Rhoden, 61
Stolen Bases: Henderson, 41	Strikeouts: Rhoden, 107

AL East
BOSTON RED SOX
1987 Finish: Fifth
1988 Prediction: Fifth

Marty Barrett

Bruce Hurst

The Red Sox are a couple of arms (a starter, a reliever) away from returning to the top of the AL East pennant chase. There are a few problems, but none that most major-league managers wouldn't swap with Bosox field boss John McNamara.

For starters, there are a pair of All-Pros in the everyday lineup. 3B Wade Boggs (.363, 24 homers), off minor knee surgery, is probably the best pure hitter in the game. Aging-but-hardly-old RF Dwight Evans (.305) remains a Boston key, offensively and defensively. Evans should be encouraged by young outfield teammates like Mike Greenwell (.328, 19 homers, 89 RBIs) and Ellis Burks (.272, 20 homers). That doesn't bode well for the future of ex-All-Pro Jim Rice. The veteran LF missed the last three weeks after sagging to .277, 13 HRs 62 RBIs.

The decline of C Rich Gedman (.205) may open the door for John Marzano (.244 in 52 games). 2B Marty Barrett is solid (.293), as is SS Spike Owen (.259, but .319 right-handed). Rookies such as SS Jody Reed and 1B Jose Birriel may fit in. Sam Horn (14 HRs in 46 games) will DH.

No one in the AL has more solid up-front starters than the Sox. Two-year Cy Young winner Roger Clemens (20–9) is the AL's best, with Bruce Hurst (15–13, despite a 1–7 finish) and Oil Can Boyd (1–3) ready to return. Rookie Danny Gabriele may be ready.

With ex-Cub fireballer Lee Smith (36 saves) on board, the weak bullpen (only 16 saves between them) no longer is. This team's 4.77 ERA was the third worst in the majors. If pitching help comes through, Sox fans can put last year's 78–84 finish (under .500 for only the second time in 20 years) in the bad-memory box.

STAT LEADERS — 1987

BATTING
Average: Boggs, .363*
Runs: Evans, 109
Hits: Boggs, 200
Doubles: Boggs, 40
Triples: Owen, 7
Home Runs: Evans, 34
RBIs: Evans, 123
Stolen Bases: Burks, 27

PITCHING
Wins: Clemens, 20**
Losses: Stanley, 15
Complete Games:
    Clemens, 18*
Shutouts: Clemens, 7*
Saves: Gardner, 10
Walks: Clemens, 83
Strikeouts: Clemens, 256

*Led league.
**Tied for league lead.

AL East
CLEVELAND INDIANS
1987 Finish: Seventh
1988 Prediction: Sixth

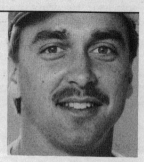

Julio Franco   **Brook Jacoby**

It will be years before anyone allows *Sports Illustrated* to forget its selection, before the '87 season, of the Indians as the AL's best team. It will be even longer before the Indians are in a position to challenge.

The preseason optimism made Cleveland's worst-in-the-majors 61–101 record even more painful. For '88, there's lots of power in the lineup, but the pitching is so poor that Manager Doc Edwards can't hope for much.

Catching is in fair shape, with Brian Dorsett (.273 in five games) getting a shot against Andy Allanson (.266) and Chris Bando (.218). Improvement is needed here. 3B Brook Jacoby has learned the strike zone, as his .300 and 32-homer season shows. He could be trade bait for a pitcher. SS Julio

Franco (career high .319) played well despite elbow problems. Pat Tabler is the Tribe's top clutch performer, with a .307 average and 34 doubles. Young Tommy Hinzo might have a shot at 2B.

Cory Snyder, Mel Hall, and Joe Carter give the Indians enough strength to wheel and deal (and ex-Oriole boss Hank Peters, the new Indian president, may do it). Snyder had 33 homers and 82 RBIs in his first full big-league season. Hall hit .280 with 18 homers and 76 RBIs. Carter set career highs in a bunch of offensive categories, including 32 homers and 106 RBIs. Free-agent Brett Butler is off to San Francisco.

Pitching, of course, is something else. Cleveland's 5.28 team ERA was the worst in the majors in *31 years!* That's sad. While Cleveland has some talented youngsters in the farm system, only righty Mike Murphy is a pitcher. If Greg Swindell bounces back from a sore elbow, things may be a little better. But look for a bunch of new faces on Indian moundsmen in '88. Hopeless?

STAT LEADERS — 1987

BATTING	PITCHING
Average: Franco, .319	Wins: Bailes, Candiotti, 7
Runs: Butler, 91	Losses: Candiotti, 18
Hits: Tabler, 170	Complete Games:
Doubles: Tabler, 34	Candiotti, 7
Triples: Butler, 8	Shutouts: Candiotti, 2
Home Runs: Snyder, 33	Saves: Jones, 8
RBIs: Carter, 106	Walks: Candiotti, 93
Stolen Bases: Butler, 33	Strikeouts: Candiotti, 111

AL East
BALTIMORE ORIOLES
1987 Finish: Sixth
1988 Prediction: Seventh

Mike Boddicker

Eddie Murray

After the Baltimore Orioles went 18–60 against the AL East last year (the worst intradivision record since division play began 19 seasons back), owner Edward Bennett Williams got out his broom. He swept out his entire front office, starting with General Manager Hank Peters (now with Cleveland).

Williams, a noted lawyer, might have started with whoever told him to give up draft choices for free agents five years earlier. The results have been a disaster. The Birds have lots of offense, little pitching, poor outfield defense, and not much help in the farm system. The road back will be long.

Manager Cal Ripken will likely have another year in charge. Fortunately, he'll have his sons, Cal, Jr., at shortstop and Billy at second base. Young Cal is only the second major-league shortstop in history with 20 or more homers for six straight years. Billy, brought up from Rochester in July, started 58 straight games until an ankle injury sidelined him. 1B Eddie Murray (.277, 91 RBIs) enjoyed his fifth 30-homer season. Trading Murray could produce several players who could help Baltimore rebound. C Terry Kennedy (.250) is solid. Larry Sheets (.316) had 31 club-high homers and is probably the most valuable Oriole.

Pitching, long the Oriole strength, is in sorry shape. Rookie righties John Habyan and Jose Mesa may each get a shot. Rookies started 63 games for the 0's last year and the team ERA (5.01) ranked 25th in the majors. Only Mike Boddicker (10–12) and Eric Bell (10–13) were healthy throughout the season. Relief ace Tom Niedenfuer (3–5, 13 saves) needs help. Improved pitching and defense will help immensely.

STAT LEADERS — 1987

BATTING
Average: Sheets, .316
Runs: C. Ripken, 97
Hits: Murray, 171
Doubles:
   Murray, C. Ripken, 28
Triples: Three with 3
Home Runs: Sheets, 31
RBIs: C. Ripken, 98
Stolen Bases: Wiggins, 20

PITCHING
Wins: Three with 10
Losses: Bell, 13
Complete Games:
   Boddicker, 7
Shutouts:
   Boddicker, Schmidt, 2
Saves: Niedenfuer, 13
Walks: Boddicker, Bell, 78
Strikeouts: Boddicker, 152

AL West
OAKLAND ATHLETICS
1987 Finish: Third
1988 Prediction: First

Dave Stewart   **Jose Canseco**

In the AL West, where anything can happen (the champion Twins would have finished fifth in the AL East), the Athletics always seem to be a couple of players away from the top, even with young talents like Mark McGwire and Jose Canseco.

1B McGwire may well be the most exciting slugger to come along in years. He destroyed the old rookie homer record with his league-leading 49 round-trippers and, unlike most young blasters, he still managed to hit .289. LF-DH Canseco enjoyed a second-straight outstanding performance (.257, 31 homers). There's more power from 2B Tony Bernazard (.250, 14 homers), RF Dave Parker (26 HRs, 97 RBIs for Cincy), and 3B Carney Lansford (.289, 19 homers). Free-agent Mike Davis is off to L.A.

Second base is still a problem area for Manager Tony LaRussa, and he could certainly use another power-hitting outfielder. LF Luis Polonia, only 5–8 and 155 pounds, hit .289 but with only 30 extra-base blows. With Alfredo Griffin off to L.A., Walt Weiss, who hit .462 in 16 late-season games, starts at short.

Ex-Dodger Bob Welch takes over as the No. 1 starter. Big righty Dave Stewart became a super pitcher in '87 (20–13, sharing the league lead in victories; 3.68; 205 strikeouts). After that, there isn't much. Moose Haas and Joaquin Andujar were free agents. Curt Young (13–7) and Steve Ontiveros (10–8) should fit it. The bullpen was a problem area. Ex-Dodger Matt Young may help.

The farm system, never baseball's strongest, has little to offer after Weiss. Hang in, Oakland.

STAT LEADERS — 1987

BATTING
Average: McGwire, .289
Runs: McGwire, 97
Hits: Canseco, 162
Doubles: Canseco, 35
Triples: Polonia, 10
Home Runs: McGwire, 49*
RBIs: McGwire, 118
Stolen Bases: Polonia, 29

PITCHING
Wins: Stewart, 20**
Losses: Stewart, 13
Complete Games:
   Stewart, 8
Shutouts:
   Stewart, Ontiveros, 1
Saves: Eckersley, Howell, 16
Walks: Stewart, 105
Strikeouts: Stewart, 205

*Led league.
**Tied for league lead.

AL West
KANSAS CITY ROYALS
1987 Finish: Second
1988 Prediction: Second

Willie Wilson

Charlie Liebrandt

We can't remember the last time that the Kaycee Royals weren't among the favorites in the AL West. The streak continues. There's plenty of talent on the Royal roster, though new manager John Wathan has some problem spots, including shortstop, catcher, and the bullpen.

Start with exciting rookie 3B Kevin Seitzer (.323, 83 RBIs), who might have been Rookie of the Year in any year that did not contain Mark McGwire and Matt Nokes. Overall, Seitzer had an AL high 207 hits, including six in one game against Boston. Danny Tartabull had 64 extra-base hits and 101 RBIs on the way to a .309 season. All-timer (now at 1B) George Brett (.290) missed 47 games. A healthy Brett is the key to Kaycee's '88 success. CF Willie Wilson slipped to .279 with only 37 extra-base blows.

If Bo Jackson decides that his future rests with the L.A. Raiders, he'll be missed by AL pitchers. (Bo fanned 158 times last year.) 2B Frank White (.245) remains solid. Still, the need to find a sound shortstop and catcher could hamper the Royals' attempts to return to the top of the division. Ex-Red Kurt Stillwell could be the answer at short.

The mound staff will miss Danny Jackson (dealt to Cincinnati). And Bret Saberhagen (18–10) will have to prove that his awful second half last year was only a momentary problem. Charlie Leibrandt (16–11) enjoyed his second-best record ever and a career high three shutouts. Ted Power (Reds) and Floyd Bannister (White Sox) will help.

The bullpen used to be Dan Quisenberry and friends. Now Quiz has had it (only eight saves last year), and guys like Gene Garber and Jerry Don Gleaton have to take over. John Davis (5–2, 2.27) is a future star.

STAT LEADERS — 1987

BATTING
Average: Seitzer, .323
Runs: Seitzer, 105
Hits: Seitzer, 207*
Doubles: Seitzer, 33
Triples: Wilson, 15
Home Runs: Tartabull, 34
RBIs: Tartabull, 101
Stolen Bases: Wilson, 59

PITCHING
Wins: Saberhagen, 18
Losses: Gubicza, D. Jackson, 18
Complete Games:
    Saberhagen, 15
Shutouts: Saberhagen, 4
Saves: Garber, Quisenberry, 8
Walks: Gubicza, 120
Strikeouts: Gubicza, 166

*Led league.

AL West
MINNESOTA TWINS
1987 Finish: First
1988 Prediction: Third

Kent Hrbek   **Gary Gaetti**

If the AL would allow the Minnesota Twins to play all their games in the Metrodome, we could guarantee the winner of the AL West title. The Twins simply do not lose at home (right, Whitey Herzog?) and hardly win on the road, something that Manager Tom Kelly will have to correct if his team is to return to the World Series.

But the World Champs have enough talent to win again. Everybody knows CF Kirby Puckett, the Twin leader on and off the field. The All-Pro hit .332 with 28 homers and 99 RBIs but saved some of his best work for defense, where he propelled his round body fast and high to rob Twin opponents of hits and homers. The guy who makes the Twins go is Gold Glove 3B Gary Gaetti (.257), the team's Mr. Clutch. 1B Kent Hrbek (.285, 34 homers) is one of the AL's best. SS Greg Gagne (.265) is solid, but the Twins could use more offense out of 2B Steve Lombardozzi (.238). LF Dan Gladden (.247) is tough, though he might not be best suited to the leadoff spot. Tom Brunansky (.259) is the main man in right. Some of the Twins' best depth comes in the outfield. The catching department is suspect, though Minny's defense is better than most people think.

The pitching-poor Boston Braves of 40 years ago had "Spahn and Sain, then two days of rain." The Twins have World Series hero Frank Viola (17–10) and aging Burt Blyleven (15–12). But thanks to their home dome, there's no chance of rain. Les Straker (8–10) couldn't be the third starter for many folks. The bullpen has Jeff Reardon (31 saves) to close, but not enough guys to set him up. It's a problem. Bryan Clarke, Don Schulze, Steve Gasser, and Jeff Bumgarner will compete for pitching jobs.

STAT LEADERS — 1987

BATTING
Average: Puckett, .332
Runs: Puckett, 96
Hits: Puckett, 207*
Doubles: Gaetti, 36
Triples: Gagne, 7
Home Runs: Hrbek, 34
RBIs: Gaetti, 109
Stolen Bases: Gladden, 25

PITCHING
Wins: Viola, 17
Losses: Blyleven, 12
Complete Games:
  Blyleven, 8
Shutouts:
  Viola, Blyleven, 1
Saves: Reardon, 31
Walks: Blyleven, 101
Strikeouts: Viola, 197

*Tied for league lead.

AL West
TEXAS RANGERS
1987 Finish: Sixth (tied)
1988 Prediction: Fourth

Ruben Sierra   **Charlie Hough**

Off a disappointing 1987 season (they were expected to challenge for the division title), the Rangers enter 1988 with a young lineup that now has had an extra year of experience. That can't hurt. Having a fine young manager like Bobby Valentine doesn't hurt either.

Best bet for future stardom in Texas? It's RF Ruben Sierra. He's the fifth player to hit 30 homers and knock in 100 runs before age 22. (Hall-of-Famers Jimmie Foxx and Mel Ott are among the others.) His .263 batting average was more than adequate. Powerful Pete Incaviglia (.271) showed improvement (27 homers, 80 RBIs). 1B Pete O'Brien (.286, 88 RBIs) was highly sought in off-season trade talks.

2B Jerry Browne (.271) seems to have his

spot nailed down, though 3B Steve Buechele (.237) spent the winter working on his hitting. Quietly, SS Scott Fletcher (.287) has moved into the group of top AL shortstops. CF Oddibe McDowell (.241) could be pressed by young Bob Brower. Ranger catchers would be in better shape if Charlie Hough wasn't on the mound staff. But Mike Stanley is improving back of the plate.

Of course, there's no telling how badly the Rangers would have done without Hough. The knuckleballer was 18–13, a career high in victories. Bobby Witt (8–10) continues to impress as does Jose Guzman (14–14). The bullpen is Dale Mohorcic (7–6, 16 saves) and a few other guys. This is a major problem area.

If Valentine tightens up his defense, finds a catcher, and keeps his pitching staff healthy, the Rangers could start climbing back. Look for Ps Brad Arnsberg, Garry Mielke, and Jose Cecena to get shots, along with OF Cecil Espy, 2B Greg Tabor, and C Chad Kreuter.

STAT LEADERS — 1987

BATTING
Average: Fletcher, .287
Runs: Sierra, 97
Hits: Fletcher, Sierra, 169
Doubles: Sierra, 35
Triples: Browne, 6
Home Runs: Parrish, 32
RBIs: Sierra, 109
Stolen Bases: Browne, 27

PITCHING
Wins: Hough, 18
Losses: Guzman, 14
Complete Games:
    Hough, 13
Shutouts: None
Saves: Mohorcic, 16
Walks: Witt, 140
Strikeouts: Hough, 223

AL West
SEATTLE MARINERS
1987 Finish: Fourth
1988 Prediction: Fifth

Alvin Davis   **Mark Langston**

Encouraged by the indoor world championship won by the AL West's Minnesota Twins, the Mariners would love to bring another title indoors to the Kingdome. They probably can't.

Not that today's M's are like the terrible old M's. Entering his last season as Seattle manager, Dick Williams has a potent offense, pretty good speed, and an improving defense. You can never count on the pitching (after ace lefty Mark Langston), and that's the trouble.

The team's .272 batting average was its best ever. Ex-Phillie powerman OF Glenn Wilson (obtained for Phil Bradley) will produce runs. OF Mickey Brantley banged the ball at a .302 clip in 92 games. 1B Alvin Davis (.295) had a career high 29 homers and knocked in 100 runs. 2B Harold Reynolds (.275) became the first No. 9 hitter to lead the league in steals (60). SS Rey Quinones (.276) and 3B Jim Presley (.247) will be pressed by Mario Diaz and Edgar Martinez. Scott Bradley (.278) and Dave Valle (.256) should again share the catching, with Mike Kingery (.280) in right, unless Williams picks up a power-hitting outfielder.

Langston (19–13, 262 league-leading strikeouts) leads the in-and-out mound crew. Ex-Oriole Ken Dixon could be a key; Mike Moore (9–19, 4.71) needs more support. Righties Mike Campbell and Clay Parker have a shot to make the '88 staff. Young Edwin Nunez did well in relief (3–4, 12 saves), along with Bill Wilkinson (3–4, 10 saves).

Though the M's probably won't win for Williams, his successor will inherit a potential champ. Look for Dave Hengel and Donell Nixon to get shots in the outfield, with Brick Smith coming on at 1B.

STAT LEADERS — 1987

BATTING
Average: P. Bradley, .297
Runs: P. Bradley, 101
Hits: P. Bradley, 179
Doubles: P. Bradley, 38
Triples: P. Bradley, 10
Home Runs: Davis, 29
RBIs: Davis, 100
Stolen Bases: Reynolds, 60*

PITCHING
Wins: Langston, 19
Losses: Moore, 19
Complete Games:
    Langston, 14
Shutouts: Langston, 3
Saves: Nunez, 12
Walks: Langston, 114
Strikeouts: Langston, 262*

*Led league.

AL West
CALIFORNIA ANGELS
1987 Finish: Sixth (tied)
1988 Prediction: Sixth

Wally Joyner   **Brian Downing**

How the mighty have fallen! Not since the 1914–15 Philadelphia Athletics (that's right, *Philadelphia*) has a team plunged from first to last in one season. That's what the '87 Angels did (actually tied for last). It doesn't seem to get a lot better in '88.

Not that the team from Disneyland is totally without talent. Maybe the Yankees and Athletics wouldn't trade for 1B Wally Joyner. But most AL folks would. Wally Wonder disproved the second-year jinx. With 117 RBIs, he became only the ninth major-leaguer ever to knock in more than 100 in each of his first two seasons. (Ted Williams and Joe DiMaggio are among the others.)

CF Devon White enjoyed a super rookie season, with 103 runs scored, 62 extra-base hits, and membership in the 20–20 club (homers and steals). Ex-Giant Chili Davis should make an instant impact.

Pitching is in fairly sorry shape, with the exceptions of righty Mike Witt (16–14, 4.01) and DeWayne Buice (8–6, 4.71). Lefty Chuck Finley (2–7) leaves the bullpen to join the starting rotation, attempting to replace John Candelaria (off to the Mets). That leaves a hole for a left-handed reliever. If righty Kirk McCaskill (4–6) bounces back, the Angels could improve.

DH Brian Downing (.272) proved to be an effective leadoff hitter. 2B Johnny Ray, obtained from Pittsburgh, could also make a difference. Jack Howell (.245) figures to get the nod at third, with Doug DeCinces gone.

There's some decent talent in the farm system that has produced Joyner and White, including outfielders Reggie Montgomery and Doug Jennings, 3B Joe Redfield, and infielders Kevin King and Bill Merrifield. Perhaps the most talented farmhand, OF Dante Bichette, is about a year away.

STAT LEADERS — 1987

BATTING
Average: Joyner, .285
Runs: Downing, 110
Hits: White, 168
Doubles: Joyner, White, 33
Triples: White, Howell, 5
Home Runs: Joyner, 34
RBIs: Joyner, 117
Stolen Bases: White, 32

PITCHING
Wins: Witt, 16
Losses: Witt, 14
Complete Games:
  Witt, 10
Shutouts: Three with 1
Saves: Buice, 17
Walks: Witt, 84
Strikeouts: Witt, 192

AL West
CHICAGO WHITE SOX
1987 Finish: Fifth
1988 Prediction: Seventh

Ozzie Guillen

Ivan Calderon

The guys who play at baseball's oldest park (Comiskey) aren't bad. It's just that they aren't very good. Manager Jim Fregosi can be proud of his mound staff (particularly the starters), his defense, and even some of his lefty hitters who can power the ball a long way.

Unfortunately, that combination of talent was only good for 77 wins in '87, which produced an unsatisfactory fifth-place finish. For '88, things could be a bit worse, but any improvement can produce surprising results in the balanced AL West.

Floyd Bannister is gone to Kaycee (for four minor-leaguers). And with Richard Dotson (11–12) off to the Yankees (for slugger Dan Pasqua), Fregosi will have to rely more on Jose DeLeon (11–12, 4.02), a hard-luck pitcher throughout his career, and Bill Long (8–8, 4.37). Righty Bobby Thigpen has become the ace of the Sox bullpen (7–5, 16 saves, 2.73). One-time bullpen leader Bob James (4–6, 10 saves) is an able backup. Pitching is highly doubtful.

Offensively, there's plenty of punch with surprising OF Ivan Calderon (.293, 38 doubles, 28 homers, 83 RBIs) and Harold Baines (.293, 20 homers, 93 RBIs). 1B Greg Walker continues to powder the ball (27 homers, 94 RBIs), and C-DH Carlton Fisk (.256, 23 homers) still does well at age 40. SS Ozzie Guillen (.279) is steady and sometimes spectacular. Rookies like 2B Fred Manrique (.258) and CF Ken Williams (.281) made an instant impact. Fregosi will probably seek a new leadoff man because Guillen and OF Gary Redus (.236, 52 steals) couldn't get it done.

Though improved hitting is a must (the Chisox finished 13th in the league), watch for right-handers Jack McDowell and Tony Menendez to get a shot this spring.

STAT LEADERS — 1987

BATTING
Average: Calderon, .293
Runs: Calderon, 93
Hits: Calderon, 159
Doubles: Calderon, 38
Triples: Guillen, 7
Home Runs: Calderon, 28
RBIs: Walker, 94
Stolen Bases: Redus, 52

PITCHING
Wins: Bannister, 16
Losses: DeLeon, Dotson, 12
Complete Games:
  Bannister, 11
Shutouts: Three with 2
Saves: Thigpen, 16
Walks: DeLeon, 97
Strikeouts: DeLeon, 153

The Mets need another super season from
ace right-hander Dwight Gooden to return
to their 1986 World Championship form.

58

National League
TEAM PREVIEWS

NL East
NEW YORK METS
1987 Finish: Second
1988 Prediction: First

 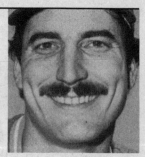

Darryl Strawberry   **Keith Hernandez**

On paper, the Mets should have won the NL East title last year. Despite their many problems, they had every opportunity to take it all — and they didn't. On paper, they should win it in 1988. Games, however, are played on real or plastic grass, and that's where championships are won.

The Mets have their share of turmoil, beginning with office boss Frank Cashen and field boss Davey Johnson. Assuming their problems don't interfere with the team, the Mets will continue to feature the game's best pitching staff (when healthy), good power, good hitting. The only major question mark: team defense.

Fireballer Dwight Gooden (15–7) seems to have bounced back fully from his winter '87 problems. Bob Ojeda (3–5) appeared to be in good shape when he returned to action late last season. A September injury sidelined super righty Ron Darling (12–8), but should be ready to go. The Met bullpen, a major headache, should be in decent shape with Roger McDowell (7–5, 25 saves) and Randy Myers (3–6), but Terry Leach will never duplicate his 11–1 season. John Candelaria or Sid Fernandez will also make it.

1B Keith Hernandez is still solid (.290, Gold Glove), but there are defensive problems at 2B (Wally Backman or Tim Teufel) and SS (Kevin Elster). Power sensation Howard Johnson (.265, 36 homers) returns at 3B despite a so-so glove. 3B Dave Magadan (.318) can hit, but his glove is suspect.

The outfield is super. Darryl Strawberry (.284, 39 homers, 104 RBIs) has blossomed into the superstar everyone thought he'd be. Quiet Kevin McReynolds (.276, 29 homers) is excellent, and Len Dykstra (.285, 37 doubles) should be the regular CF. There's lots of young talent, too. The Mets will have to replace aging C Gary Carter soon.

STAT LEADERS — 1987

BATTING
Average: Hernandez, .290
Runs: Strawberry, 108
Hits: Hernandez, 170
Doubles: Dykstra, 37
Triples: Wilson, 7
Home Runs: Strawberry, 39
RBIs: Strawberry, 104
Stolen Bases: Strawberry, 36

PITCHING
Wins: Gooden, 15
Losses: Orosco, 9
Complete Games: Gooden, 7
Shutouts: Gooden, 3
Saves: McDowell, 25
Walks: Darling, 96
Strikeouts: Darling, 167

NL East
MONTREAL EXPOS
1987 Finish: Third
1988 Prediction: Second

Bryn Smith

Mitch Webster

In the surprising NL East (surprise winners and surprise losers), no team surprised more than the Montreal Expos. Expected to finish near the bottom, the '87 Expos were in the pennant race three days before the season ended.

Now, Manager Buck Rodgers, what do you do for an encore? It may be tough. First, the Expos will sneak up on no one. Unlike Rodney Dangerfield, they get plenty of respect. Name a better LF than Tim Raines? You can't. Raines (.330, despite missing the first month of the season) finished among the league leaders in just about every offensive department. And Timothy covers acres of ground on defense.

SS Hubie Brooks bounced back from a fractured right wrist to hit 14 homers (most by an NL SS) and knocked in 29 runs in September. Rumors of a move to right field have Brooks crying the blues. But he'll be a star anywhere he plays. 3B Tim Wallach is the NL's best, now that Mike Schmidt is 38. Wallach banged in 123 runs, tops by an NL 3B since 1971, and led the majors with 42 doubles. 1B Andres Galarraga hit .305 and is a superb fielder. Casey Candaele does well wherever he plays —and that means six positions. Mitch Webster (101 runs) and Herm Winningham join Raines in the out-field most of the time. Catching is a major problem area, as it is for most teams these days.

Pitching will be decent, if not deep. Den-nis Martinez (11–4, 3.30) and Pasqual Perez (7–10, 2.30 in September) lifted a staff that featured Neal Heaton and Bryn Smith. The recovery of Floyd Youmans from drug prob-lems will help. Tim Burke, Andy McGaffigan, and Bob McClure run a bull-pen by committee.

STAT LEADERS — 1987

BATTING

Average: Raines, .330
Runs: Raines, 123
Hits: Wallach, 177
Doubles: Wallach, 42*
Triples: Raines, Webster, 8
Home Runs: Wallach, 26
RBIs: Wallach, 123
Stolen Bases: Raines, 50

PITCHING

Wins: Heaton, 13
Losses: Sebra, 15
Complete Games:
    Sebra, 4
Shutouts: Youmans, 3
Saves: St. Claire, 7
Walks: Sebra, 67
Strikeouts: Sebra, 156

*Led league.

NL East
ST. LOUIS CARDINALS
1987 Finish: First
1988 Prediction: Third

Todd Worrell   **Tom Herr**

You certainly can't call the Cardinals lucky. Despite losing star pitcher John Tudor for half a season with a freak injury; losing Jack Clark, the team's only powerman, for the stretch drive, play-offs, and World Series; and an off-year for expensive catcher Tony Pena, the Cards came within a whisker of winning the world title.

With good health (all the key pitchers lost time last year), the Redbirds will be right in the thick of things again this year. (Remember, no divisional champ has repeated in the 1980s!) Tudor (10–2), Danny Cox (11–9), Joe Magrane (9–7), and Greg Mathews (11–11) are the keys to a lot of victories. And when they turn a lead over to ace reliever Todd Worrell (33 saves), victory is almost certain.

Despite missing most of the last month (will he ever have a healthy season?), 1B Jack Clark (.286, 35 homers, 106 RBIs) remains one of the NL's most feared hitters. He was walked 136 times last year, tops in the NL. MVP runner-up SS Ozzie Smith (.303) is simply the best there is and, with 2B Tommy Herr (.263), provides excellent middle defense. 3B Terry Pendleton (.286), whose ninth-inning homer crushed the Mets last year, is solid.

The outfield features two of the quickest humans ever to play the game. Vincent Coleman (.289, 109 steals) and Willie McGee (.285) track down everything hit in their neighborhood. Platoon RF Jim Lindeman, who suffered with back ills last year, should be healthy and in the lineup everyday, adding power to the Card lineup. With his new glasses, Tony Pena (.214) should bounce back to his All-Pro form. Pitchers Scott Terry, Cris Carpenter, and Rich Buonantony could help.

STAT LEADERS — 1987

BATTING
Average: Smith, .303
Runs: Coleman, 121
Hits: Smith, 182
Doubles: Smith, 40
Triples: McGee, 11
Home Runs: Clark, 35
RBIs: Clark, 106
Stolen Bases: Coleman, 109*

PITCHING
Wins: Three with 11
Losses: Mathews, 11
Complete Games: Magrane, 4
Shutouts: Magrane, 2
Saves: Worrell, 33
Walks: Cox, Mathews, 71
Strikeouts: Mathews, 108

*Led league.

NL East
PHILADELPHIA PHILLIES
1987 Finish: Fourth (tied)
1988 Prediction: Fourth

Mike Schmidt

Steve Bedrosian

As Mike Schmidt signed his new (his last?) multimillion-buck contract, he stated firmly, "We'll be there in '88!" By "there," ol' Michael Jack meant the NL East pennant race. We don't agree.

Manager Lee Elia certainly has the talent to win. His biggest job is to make the Phils play hard just about everyday. Schmidt, even at age 38, owns a super bat (.293, 35 homers, 113 RBIs). As long as his aching knees allow him to walk, he'll hit a ton. All-Pro 2B Juan Samuel (.272, 28 homers, 100 RBIs) ranks with the most exciting players in the game. He simply must reduce his strikeouts (162 last year). Speedy OF Milt Thompson (.302, 46 steals) joins Samuel in providing whatever speed the club has. Ex-Cub OF Bob Dernier, signed as a free agent, will help. 1B Von Hayes (.277, 21 homers, 84 RBIs) disappointed somewhat in '87, but he is a solid pro.

Reliable ex-Mariner OF Phil Bradley arrives with speed and a .297 bat. (Glenn Wilson went to Seattle.) SS Steve Jeltz (.232) will probably be back in the lineup. Perhaps baseball's premier pinch hitter is Greg Gross, who batted 133 times in 114 games (and hit .286!). Expensive C Lance Parrish (.245) must return to his old Tiger form — or else! (They're very tough in Philly!)

Consistency is the key to the mound staff. Cy Young Award winner Steve Bedrosian (5–3, 40 saves) is the "bedrock" of the bullpen. But the starters and middle relievers will have to set him up. Kevin Gross (9–16), Don Carman (13–11), and Bruce Ruffin (11–14) are excellent *some* of the time. Shane Rawley (17–11) is excellent *most* of the time. Farm-system righties Tom Newell, Bob Scanlan, and Marvin Freeman could help soon.

STAT LEADERS — 1987

BATTING
Average: Thompson, .302
Runs: Samuel, 113
Hits: Samuel, 178
Doubles: Samuel, 37
Triples: Samuel, 15*
Home Runs: Schmidt, 35
RBIs: Schmidt, 113
Stolen Bases: Thompson, 46

PITCHING
Wins: Rawley, 17
Losses: K. Gross, 16
Complete Games:
  Rawley, 4
Shutouts: Carman, 2
Saves: Bedrosian, 40*
Walks: K. Gross, 87
Strikeouts: Carman, 125

*Led League.

NL East
PITTSBURGH PIRATES
1987 Finish: Fourth (tied)
1988 Prediction: Fifth

Andy Van Slyke

Mike LaValliere

You know your team is on the road to success when the president and the general manager are fighting for control. That's what happened in Pittsburgh this winter, and the winner was GM Syd Thrift. Why not? He has this long-suffering club on the way up.

The Pirates may well have the best young pitchers in the NL. Sensational rookie Mike Dunne shocked his old club (the Cards) by going 13–6 with a 3.03 ERA (second in the league), and was even hotter (10–2) in the late going. A pair of ex-Yanks, Doug Drabek (11-12, 3.88) and Brian Fisher (11-9), provide additional hope. Veteran Bob Walk (8–2, 3.31) will probably remain in the starting rotation with Jim Gott and Don Robinson the key men in the bullpen.

Like most good teams, Pittsburgh's

strength is up the middle. Another ex-Card (via the Tony Pena trade), catcher Mike LaValliere, hit .300 and is solid on defense. Jose Lind played well enough (.322 in 35 games) for the Bucs to move ex-All Pro Johnny Ray. The Pirates will have to find a DP partner for Lind from among Al Pedrique, Felix Fermin, and Rafael Belliard. (Pittsburgh employed nine shortstops last year!) Barry Bonilla will see plenty of action at third or in the outfield, with the Pirates looking for more power from Sid Bream — or whoever else lands at 1B.

Andy Van Slyke, who also arrived in the Pena deal, was a stickout in CF, hitting .293 with 21 round-trippers. LF Barry Bonds (.261, 77 RBIs) has great power potential.

Pittsburgh has enough depth in the farm system to trade name players for the players they need. Watch for P Tim Drummond and catchers Mackey Sasser and Tom Prince to get a full spring shot. P Logan Easley, though released in November, may be back.

STAT LEADERS — 1987

BATTING
Average: Bonilla, .300
Runs: Bonds, 99
Hits: Van Slyke, 165
Doubles: Van Slyke, 36
Triples: Van Slyke, 11
Home Runs: Bonds, 25
RBIs: Van Slyke, 82
Stolen Bases: Van Slyke, 34

PITCHING
Wins: Dunne, 13
Losses: Drabek, 12
Complete Games:
  Fisher, 6
Shutouts: Fisher, 3
Saves: J. Robinson, 14
Walks: Fisher, 72
Strikeouts: Drabek, 120

NL East
CHICAGO CUBS
1987 Finish: Sixth
1988 Prediction: Sixth

Ryne Sandberg

Jerry Mumphrey

Blessed with the NL's Most Valuable Player (Andre Dawson) and a Cy Young contender (Rick Sutcliffe), the 1987 Cubs still managed to finish in the NL East cellar. Despite major management changes (front office and dugout), long-suffering Chicago fans may continue to suffer in '88. Sorry about that, Manager Don Zimmer.

Things are particularly tough in the bullpen where Lee "36 Saves" Smith is gone to Boston in a strange deal. Ex-Sox Al Nipper and Calvin Schiraldi will fill two roster spots. Sutcliffe (18–10, 3.68) is just about it in the starting department. Rookie righty Les Lancaster was 8–3, but with a 4.90 ERA. Bob Tewksbury (0–4) must bounce back from a sore arm.

Offense isn't a major problem in Chicago. RF Dawson (.287, 49 homers, 137 RBIs) is a superstar (OK, an underpaid superstar). The Cubs were going fairly well until 2B Ryne Sandberg (.294) went down with an ankle injury early in the season. Re-signing free-agent vet OF Jerry Mumphrey (.333) was a major off-season accomplishment. 3B Keith Moreland (.266, 27 homers, 88 RBIs) is a defensive liability, but solid on offense. Moreland and 1B Leon Durham (27 homers, only 63 RBIs) are both tradable. Though C Jody Davis (.248) battled with ex-Cub boss Dallas Green, he remains one of the best. IF Paul Noce (.228) may try to pinch-hit in '88, and SS Shawon Dunston (.246) should continue to improve. Free-agent OF Bob Dernier (.317) is now a Phillie, but there's plenty of stickwork from Dave Martinez (.292) and Manny Trillo (.294).

Help may be on the way, with first sacker Mark Grace and outfielders Dwight Smith and Rolando Roomes.

STAT LEADERS — 1987

BATTING
Average: Sandberg, .294
Runs: Dawson, 90
Hits: Dawson, 178
Doubles: Moreland, 29
Triples: Martinez, 8
Home Runs: Dawson, 49*
RBIs: Dawson, 137*
Stolen Bases: Sandberg, 21

PITCHING
Wins: Sutcliffe, 18
Losses: Moyer, 15
Complete Games:
   Sutcliffe, 6
Shutouts: Trout, 2
Saves: Smith, 36
Walks: Sutcliffe, 106
Strikeouts: Sutcliffe, 174

*Led league.

NL West
HOUSTON ASTROS
1987 Finish: Third
1988 Prediction: First

Bill Doran

Nolan Ryan

Though the Astros tumbled from the top of the NL West to a 76–86 record, there's every reason to believe that Houston will be back in the West chase again in '88. Manager Hal Lanier, with more power than ever, has a solid pitching core, an excellent basic lineup, and good defense.

You have to wonder how long 41-year-old Nolan Ryan can continue to baffle NL hitters. Hard-luck Nolan went 8–16, despite a league-leading 2.76 ERA (and 270 strikeouts); he remains a pitching marvel. Mike Scott, no matter what he's throwing, still frightens NL batters, though he slumped to 16–13 and 3.23. Jim Deshaies (11–6, 4.62) is an outstanding No. 3 man. Dave Smith (2–3, 1.65, 24 saves) remains one of the NL's top closers, though the Astros could certainly use a lefty in the 'pen to work with him. The Astro mound staff was third in the league a year ago, and pitching remains the key.

The top of Lanier's lineup is superb. CF Gerald Young (.321), one of five switch-hitters in the 'Stros' everyday order, shows great potential. LF Billy Hatcher (.296) has some power. 2B Billy Doran (.283), another switcher, is among the NL's top second sackers year after year. 3B Ken Caminiti (.246, but .310 right-handed) was a pleasant surprise, especially on defense. SS Craig Reynolds (.254) should return, and ex-Brave Rafael Ramirez arrives. 1B Glenn Davis (.251, 27 homers) must turn up the power for the Astros to bounce back. RF Kevin Bass (.284) is outstanding in the field, too. C Alan Ashby's arm has seen better days, but the guy can hit (.288, 14 HRs). Lanier is looking for a lefty power man and some depth at catcher. Ps Manny Hernandez and Rob Mallicoat, SS Chuck Jackson, and C Craig Biggio could help.

STAT LEADERS — 1987

BATTING
Average: Hatcher, .296
Runs: Hatcher, 96
Hits: Doran, 177
Doubles: Davis, 35
Triples: Bass, 5
Home Runs: Davis, 27
RBIs: Davis, 93
Stolen Bases: Hatcher, 53

PITCHING
Wins: Scott, 16
Losses: Knepper, 17
Complete Games:
 Scott, 8
Shutouts: Scott, 3
Saves: Smith, 24
Walks: Ryan, 87
Strikeouts: Ryan, 270*

*Led league.

NL West
SAN FRANCISCO GIANTS
1987 Finish: First
1988 Prediction: Second

Jeffrey Leonard

Mike Aldrete

Only the Cardinals (who upset the surprising Giants on their way to the World Series) and the voters of San Francisco (who failed to approve a new stadium for the ball club) could spoil a great season by the Bay.

With a combination of young veterans and new players obtained in cagey trades by front-office boss Al Rosen, Manager Roger Craig's Giants zoomed right to the top of the NL West.

The biggest uncertainty is where the Giants will play after their lease at Candlestick Park expires in 1994. Meanwhile, there's plenty of talent to bring joy to the windy field at the current location. The infield is solid, offensively and defensively. 1B Will Clark (.308, 35 homers, 91 RBIs) is among the NL's best. 3B Kevin

Mitchell (.280, 22 homers, 70 RBIs) was a great midseason pickup, though Matt Williams may push him to the OF. SS Jose Uribe (.291) is first-rate, and Rob Thompson (.262) is solid. The outfield is tops, led by No. 00 Jeffrey Leonard (.280), surprising Candy Maldonado (.292, 85 RBIs), ex-Indian Brett Butler, and hard-hitting Mike Aldrete (.325). Speedy Eddie Milner is ready.

Though the Giants lack a great No. 1 pitcher, Rich Reuschel won 6 of 9 at San Francisco and will fill that role for now. He and Mike Krukow (5–6) are aging, and Atlee Hammaker (10–10) has a history of arm woes, so Craig is looking for starting pitching. Scott Garrelts (11–7, 12 saves) will likely replace Don Robinson (11–7, 19 saves) as the bullpen stopper. Their major advantage: C Bob Brenly (.267), possibly the NL's top defensive catcher.

STAT LEADERS — 1987

BATTING
Average: Clark, .308*
Runs: Clark, 89
Hits: Clark, 163
Doubles: Clark, Leonard, 29
Triples: Three with 5
Home Runs: Clark, 35
RBIs: Clark, 91
Stolen Bases: Three with 16

PITCHING
Wins: LaCoss, 13
Losses: Hammacker, LaCoss, 10
Complete Games: Downs, 4**
Shutouts: Downs, 3**
Saves: D. Robinson, 19
Walks: Downs, 67
Strikeouts: Downs, 137

*Aldrete (.325 in 357 at-bats) did not qualify.
**Reuschel, who split the season between Pittsburgh and SF, shared league lead in complete games and shutouts.

NL West
CINCINNATI REDS
1987 Finish: Second
1988 Prediction: Third

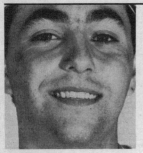 

John Franco   Eric Davis

Normally, a second-place finish is cheered by hopeful fans looking forward to an even better performance the following season. Not so in Cincinnati, where the Reds were expecting to finish first and where owner Marge Schott seems to be causing as many problems as Boss George.

Even Manager Pete Rose isn't on firm ground starting the '88 campaign. He has a powerful lineup but too little pitching (ex-Royal Danny Jackson will help). But the Cincy locker room isn't the best place to hang out, and the trainer's table is too often the most popular place in town.

No doubt that CF Eric Davis (.293, 37 homers, 100 RBIs) is one of the NL's top players. But his game-focus is sometimes fuzzy. Kal Daniels (.334, 26 homers) is outstanding. RF Dave Parker (.253) is gone to Oakland (for Ps Jose Rijo and Tim Birtsas).

1B Nick Esasky (.272) gets help from infield youngsters like SS Barry Larkin (.244) and late-arriving 2B Jeff Treadway (.333 in 23 games). Dave Concepcion is the vet in the group, now that Kurt Stillwell is off to Kansas City. C Bo Diaz, a former All-Pro, also fell victim to a second-half slump in '87, finishing at .270. Though Ron Oester is gone, Paul O'Neill (.256) will provide depth.

The late-season addition of ex-Yank Dennis Rasmussen (and the ex-As) will help the poor starting pitching staff. Tom Browning (10–13, but 5.02) will be back along with Guy Hoffman (9–10), coming off surgery. The bullpen is in great shape (how about that, Pete?) with ace fireman John Franco (8–5, 2.52, 32 saves) heading the crew. Jeff Gray could join him with Pat Pacillo and Jack Armstrong trying for a starting berth.

STAT LEADERS — 1987

BATTING
Average: Davis, .293*
Runs: Davis, 120
Hits: Parker, 149
Doubles: Davis, 35
Triples: Stillwell, 7
Home Runs: Davis, 37
RBIs: Davis, 100
Stolen Bases: Davis, 50

PITCHING
Wins: Three with 10
Losses: Power, Browning, 13
Complete Games:
  Gullickson, 3
Shutouts: Power,
  Gullickson, 1
Saves: Franco, 32
Walks: Power, 71
Strikeouts: Power, 133

*Daniels (.334 in 368 at-bats) did not qualify.

NL West
SAN DIEGO PADRES
1987 Finish: Sixth
1988 Prediction: Fourth

Garry Templeton   **Marvell Wynne**

The Padres have to be the most optimistic last-place team in baseball. After the worst start in the majors a year ago, San Diego's outstanding young talent was competitive over the last three months. If the pitching and power improve, this club is on the way up.

You can hardly miss when you lead off with All-Pro RF Tony Gwynn (league-leading .370, 218 hits). The middle of the lineup is bolstered by 1B John Kruk (.313, 91 RBIs) and the NL's top catcher (at age 23) Benito Santiago (.300, including a 34-game hit streak). Manager Larry Bowa must find a regular spot for IF Randy Ready (.309), who split time at second and third a year ago. Unfortunately, one-time All-Pro SS Garry Templeton's offense has sputtered (.222).

In addition to Gwynn, Marvell Wynne (.250), Shane Mack (.239), and trade-candidate Carmelo Martinez (.273) will man the outfield until Stan Jefferson (.230) and Shawn Abner (.300 at Las Vegas) are ready to go.

The mound staff will have to improve for the Padres to get into the thick of things. Eric Show (8–16) is still the ace (most of the time), with Ed Whitson (10–13) last year's top winner. Young Eric Nolte (2–6, but 3.21) pitched better than his record indicates. And Jimmy Jones (9–7) could be a star of the future.

The bullpen needs help, too, led by inconsistent Lance McCullers (8–10) and a fading Goose Gossage (5–4). Mark Davis, obtained from the Giants, had a 2.02 ERA over his last 24 appearances.

Watch for the Alomar boys (C Sandy, Jr., and IF Roberto), both of whom topped .300 at Las Vegas. Some scouts say that young Sandy could be even better than Santiago!

STAT LEADERS — 1987

BATTING
Average: Gwynn, .370*
Runs: Gwynn, 119
Hits: Gwynn, 218*
Doubles: Gwynn, 36
Triples: Gwynn, 13
Home Runs: Kruk, 20
RBIs: Kruk, 91
Stolen Bases: Gwynn, 56

PITCHING
Wins: Whitson, 10
Losses: Show, 16
Complete Games: Show, 5
Shutouts: Show, 3
Saves: McCullers, 16
Walks: Show, 85
Strikeouts: Whitson, 135

*Led league.

NL West
LOS ANGELES DODGERS
1987 Finish: Fourth
1988 Prediction: Fifth

Fernando Valenzuela   **Steve Sax**

These are the worst of times in L.A. No, we're not talking about the famous earthquake. We're talking about the Dodgers, another L.A. disaster area. Despite an outstanding starting trio of pitchers, the men of Tom Lasorda are sinking fast in the West, and help doesn't seem to be on the way.

If Lasorda eats to forget his troubles, he'll soon burst out of his Dodger blues. He'll miss Bob Welch (15–9, 3.22, league-leading four shutouts), but Orel Hershiser (16–16, 3.06, 10 complete games) and screwballing lefty Fernando Valenzuela (14–14, 3.98, 12 complete games, 190 strikeouts) are super. Fact is, the Dodgers' 3.72 team ERA trailed only West champion San Francisco. The rest of the staff was quite ordinary. The bullpen, led by Alejandro Pena (2–7, 11 saves), was awful. Ex-Met Jesse Orosco and ex-Athletic Jay Howell must bounce back.

Elsewhere, L.A. was trouble city. Certainly Pedro Guerrero, in left or at first base, is among the NL's very best. He finished second in hitting (.338), hit 27 homers, and knocked in 89 runs, showing complete recovery from his knee injury of '86. If CF John Shelby (.277, 69 RBIs) is for real, he's a big plus. Ex-Athletic Mike Davis will help. But RF Mike Marshall (.294) is always hurt, C Mike Scioscia (.265) hit only six homers, and 1B Franklin Stubbs hit only .233. Worse still, the whole ball club can't field a lick (last in the NL). One-time AL All-Pro Alfredo Griffin should fill the bill at SS. Anybody know a good 3B?

The farm system, which usually produces new Dodgers all the time, is almost bare. Look for Ken Devereaux and Chris Gwynn (brother of San Diego's Tony) to get shots in '88, along with pitchers Shawn Hillegas and Tim Crews.

STAT LEADERS — 1987

BATTING

Average: Guerrero, .338
Runs: Guerrero, 89
Hits: Guerrero, 184
Doubles: Scioscia, Shelby, 26
Triples: Stubbs, Anderson, 3
Home Runs: Guerrero, 27
RBIs: Guerrero, 89
Stolen Bases: Sax, 37

PITCHING

Wins: Hershiser, 16
Losses: Hershiser, 16
Complete Games:
    Valenzuela, 12*
Shutouts: Welch, 4*
Saves: Pena, Young, 11
Walks: Valenzuela, 124
Strikeouts: Welch, 196

*Tied for league lead.

NL West
ATLANTA BRAVES
1987 Finish: Fifth
1988 Prediction: Sixth

Dion James

Andres Thomas

The 1987 Braves were probably not as good as their 69–92 record indicates. This is a team in trouble. Atlanta hit .258 (their opponents hit .276), the team ERA of 4.63 was the NL's worst, and the bullpen started more fires than it put out. Tough numbers!

RF Dale Murphy's hefty new contract will keep the 44-homer, 105-RBI man in town for years to come. We hope he's happy. Though Rafael Ramirez is gone (Houston), there's good depth at SS with exciting Andres Thomas (.231) and Jeff Blauser (.242) doing battle. Thomas will likely move to third, freeing vet Ken Oberkfell to the trade mart. There's confusion behind the plate where vet Bruce Benedict (.147) is probably through. Ozzie Virgil (27 HRs) should start, with help from aging Ted Simmons (.277) and young

Terry Bell. 1B Gerald Perry (.270) is fine, though 2B Glenn Hubbard (.264) has slipped. CF Dion James (.312), the Braves' top hitter, is just fine, thank you, though he could move to left if a new CF is found. That fellow could be ex-Met prospect Terry Blocker (.312 at Tidewater) or Albert Hall.

The pitching staff, particularly the bullpen, needs a major overhaul. There are youngsters in the Brave organization, like Tommy Glavine, Pete Smith, Chuck Cary, and John Smoltz who should get a full examination this spring. Jim Acker (68 games, 14 saves) should return to the 'pen, with Gene Garber (10 saves). Zane Smith (15–10, nine complete games) is a major-league starter. But Rick Mahler (8–13, 4.98) and David Palmer (8–11, 4.90) will have to bounce back for the Braves to have any chance. Fortunately, Manager Chuck Tanner is great with young players. He'll have to be.

STAT LEADERS — 1987

BATTING

Average: James, .312
Runs: Murphy, 115
Hits: Murphy, 167
Doubles: James, 37
Triples: James, 6
Home Runs: Murphy, 44
RBIs: Murphy, 105
Stolen Bases: Perry, 42

PITCHING

Wins: Z. Smith, 15
Losses: Mahler, 13
Complete Games:
 Z. Smith, 9
Shutouts: Z. Smith, 3
Saves: Acker, 14
Walks: Z. Smith, 91
Strikeouts: Z. Smith, 130

The Padres may have finished last in 1987,
but with youngsters like catcher Benito
Santiago, they should contend soon.

84

STATISTICS
1987

AMERICAN LEAGUE
Batting

(30 or more at-bats)
*Bats Left-handed   †Switch-Hitter

Batter and Club	AVG	G	AB	R	H	HR	RBI	SB
Allanson, Andrew, Clev.	.266	50	154	17	41	3	16	1
Armas, Antonio, Cal.	.198	28	81	8	16	3	9	1
Baines, Harold, Chi.*	.293	132	505	59	148	20	93	0
Balboni, Stephen, K.C.	.207	121	386	44	80	24	60	0
Bando, Christopher, Clev.†	.218	89	211	20	46	5	16	0
Barfield, Jesse, Tor.	.263	159	590	89	155	28	84	3
Barrett, Martin, Bos........	.293	137	559	72	164	3	43	15
Baylor, Donald, Bos.-Minn.	.245	128	388	67	95	16	63	5
Bean, William, Det.*	.258	26	66	6	17	0	4	1
Bell, George, Tor.	.308	156	610	111	188	47	134	5
Bell, Jay, Clev.	.216	38	125	14	27	2	13	2
Beniquez, Juan, K.C.-Tor.	.251	96	255	20	64	8	47	0
Benzinger, Todd, Bos.†	.278	73	223	36	62	8	43	5
Bergman, David, Det.*......	.273	91	172	25	47	6	22	0
Bernazard, T., Clev.-Oak.†	.250	140	507	73	127	14	49	11
Biancalana, Roland, K.C.†	.213	37	47	4	10	1	7	0
Boggs, Wade, Bos.*	.363	147	551	108	200	24	89	1
Bonilla, Juan, N.Y...........	.255	23	55	6	14	1	3	0
Boone, Robert, Cal.	.242	128	389	42	94	3	33	0
Bosley, Thaddis, K.C.*......	.279	80	140	13	39	1	16	0
Boston, Daryl, Chi.*	.258	103	337	51	87	10	29	12
Bradley, Philip, Sea.	.297	158	603	101	179	14	67	40
Bradley, Scott, Sea.*	.278	102	342	34	95	5	43	0
Braggs, Glenn, Mil.	.269	132	505	67	136	13	77	12
Brantley, Michael, Sea.	.302	92	351	52	106	14	54	13
Brett, George, K.C.*	.290	115	427	71	124	22	78	6
Brock, Gregory, Mil.*	.299	141	532	81	159	13	85	5
Brookens, Thomas, Det.....	.241	143	444	59	107	13	59	7
Brower, Robert, Tex.	.261	127	303	63	79	14	46	15
Browne, Jerome, Tex.†	.271	132	454	63	123	1	38	27
Brunansky, Tom, Minn.	.259	155	532	83	138	32	85	11

Batter and Club	AVG	G	AB	R	H	HR	RBI	SB
Buckner, W., Bos.-Cal.*	.286	132	469	39	134	5	74	2
Buechele, Steven, Tex......	.237	136	363	45	86	13	50	2
Burks, Ellis, Bos.	.272	133	558	94	152	20	59	27
Burleson, Richard, Balt.	.209	62	206	26	43	2	14	0
Bush, R. Randall, Minn.*	.253	122	293	46	74	11	46	10
Butera, Salvatore, Minn. ...	.171	51	111	7	19	1	12	0
Butler, Brett, Clev.*	.295	137	522	91	154	9	41	33
Calderon, Ivan, Chi.	.293	144	542	93	159	28	83	10
Canseco, Jose, Oak.	.257	159	630	81	162	31	113	15
Carter, Joseph, Clev.	.264	149	588	83	155	32	106	31
Castillo, Juan, Mil.†	.224	116	321	44	72	3	28	15
Castillo, M., Clev.	.250	89	220	27	55	11	31	1
Cerone, Richard, N.Y.	.243	113	284	28	69	4	23	0
Cey, Ronald, Oak.	.221	45	104	12	23	4	11	0
Christensen, John, Sea.	.242	53	132	19	32	2	12	2
Clark, David, Clev.*	.207	29	87	11	18	3	12	1
Coles, Darnell, Det.	.181	53	149	14	27	4	15	0
Cooper, Cecil, Mil.*	.248	63	250	25	62	6	36	1
Cotto, Henry, N.Y.	.235	68	149	21	35	5	20	4
Davidson, Mark, Minn.	.267	102	150	32	40	1	14	9
Davis, Alvin, Sea.*	.295	157	580	86	171	29	100	0
Davis, Michael, Oak.*	.265	139	494	69	131	22	72	19
DeCinces, Doug, Cal.	.234	133	453	65	106	16	63	3
Deer, Robert, Mil.	.238	134	474	71	113	28	80	12
Dempsey, Rick, Clev.	.177	60	141	16	25	1	9	0
Dodson, Patrick, Bos.*	.167	26	42	4	7	2	6	0
Downing, Brian, Cal.	.272	155	567	110	154	29	77	5
Ducey, Robert, Tor.*	.188	34	48	12	9	1	6	2
Dwyer, James, Balt.*	.274	92	241	54	66	15	33	4
Easler, Michael, N.Y.*	.281	65	167	13	47	4	21	1
Eisenreich, James, K.C.* ...	.238	44	105	10	25	4	21	1
Evans, Darrell, Det.*	.257	150	499	90	128	34	99	6
Evans, Dwight, Bos.	.305	154	541	109	165	34	123	4
Felder, Michael, Mil.†	.266	108	289	48	77	2	31	34
Fernandez, Tony, Tor.†	.322	146	578	90	186	5	67	32
Fielder, Cecil, Tor.	.269	82	175	30	47	14	32	0
Fisk, Carlton, Chi.	.256	135	454	68	116	23	71	1

Batter and Club	AVG	G	AB	R	H	HR	RBI	SB
Fletcher, Scott, Tex.	.287	156	588	82	169	5	63	13
Franco, Julio, Clev.	.319	128	495	86	158	8	52	32
Frobel, Douglas, Clev.*	.100	29	40	5	4	2	5	0
Gaetti, Gary, Minn.	.257	154	584	95	150	31	109	10
Gagne, Gregory, Minn.	.265	137	437	68	116	10	40	6
Gallagher, David, Clev.	.111	15	36	2	4	0	1	2
Gallego, Michael, Oak.	.250	72	124	18	31	2	14	0
Gantner, James, Mil.*	.272	81	265	37	72	4	30	6
Gedman, Richard, Bos.*	.205	52	151	11	31	1	13	0
Gerhart, Ken, Balt.	.243	92	284	41	69	14	34	9
Gibson, Kirk, Det.*	.277	128	487	95	135	24	79	26
Gladden, Dan, Minn.	.249	121	438	69	109	8	38	25
Gonzales, Rene, Balt.	.267	37	60	14	16	1	7	1
Greenwell, Mike, Bos.*	.328	125	412	71	135	19	89	5
Griffin, Alfredo, Oak.†	.263	144	494	69	130	3	60	26
Grubb, John, Det.*	.202	59	114	9	23	2	13	0
Gruber, Kelly, Tor.	.235	138	341	50	80	12	36	12
Guillen, Oswaldo, Chi.*	.279	149	560	64	156	2	51	25
Hairston, Jerry, Chi.†	.230	66	126	14	29	5	20	0
Hall, Melvin, Clev.*	.280	142	485	57	136	18	76	5
Harper, Terry, Det.	.203	31	64	4	13	3	10	1
Hart, Michael, Balt.*	.158	34	76	7	12	4	12	1
Hassey, Ronald, Chi.*	.214	49	145	15	31	3	12	0
Heath, Michael, Det.	.281	93	270	34	76	8	33	1
Henderson, David, Bos.	.234	75	184	30	43	8	25	1
Henderson, Rickey, N.Y.	.291	95	358	78	104	17	37	41
Henderson, Stephen, Oak.	.289	46	114	14	33	3	9	0
Hendrick, George, Cal.	.241	65	162	14	39	5	25	0
Herndon, Larry, Det.	.324	89	225	32	73	9	47	1
Hill, Donald, Chi.†	.239	111	410	57	98	9	46	1
Hinzo, Thomas, Clev.†	.265	67	257	31	68	3	21	9
Hoffman, Glenn, Bos.	.200	21	55	5	11	0	6	0
Horn, Samuel, Bos.*	.278	46	158	31	44	14	34	0
Howell, Jack, Cal.*	.245	138	449	64	110	23	64	4
Hrbek, Kent, Minn.*	.285	143	477	85	136	34	90	5
Hulett, Timothy, Chi.	.217	68	240	20	52	7	28	0
Incaviglia, Peter, Tex.	.271	139	509	85	138	27	80	9

Batter and Club	AVG	G	AB	R	H	HR	RBI	SB
Iorg, Garth, Tor.	.210	122	310	35	65	4	30	2
Jackson, Reginald, Oak.*	.220	115	336	42	74	15	43	2
Jackson, Vincent, K.C.	.235	116	396	46	93	22	53	10
Jacoby, Brook, Clev.	.300	155	540	73	162	32	69	2
Javier, Stanley, Oak.†	.185	81	151	22	28	2	9	3
Jones, Ross, K.C.	.254	39	114	10	29	0	10	1
Jones, Ruppert, Cal.*	.245	85	192	25	47	8	28	2
Joyner, Wallace, Cal.*	.285	149	564	100	161	34	117	8
Karkovice, Ronald, Chi.	.071	39	85	7	6	2	7	3
Kearney, Robert, Sea.	.170	24	47	5	8	0	1	0
Keedy, C. Patrick, Chi.	.171	17	41	6	7	2	2	1
Kelly, Roberto, N.Y.	.269	23	52	12	14	1	7	9
Kennedy, Terry, Balt.*	.250	143	512	51	128	18	62	1
Kiefer, Steven, Mil.	.202	28	99	17	20	5	17	0
Kingery, Michael, Sea.*	.280	120	354	38	99	9	52	7
Kittle, Ronald, N.Y.	.277	59	159	21	44	12	28	0
Knight, C. Ray, Balt.	.256	150	563	46	144	14	65	0
Kunkel, Jeffrey, Tex.	.219	15	32	1	7	1	2	0
Lacy, Leondaus, Balt.	.244	87	258	35	63	7	28	3
Lansford, Carney, Oak.	.289	151	554	89	160	19	76	27
Larkin, Eugene, Minn.†	.266	85	233	23	62	4	28	1
Laudner, Timothy, Minn.	.191	113	288	30	55	16	43	1
Leach, Richard, Tor.*	.282	98	195	26	55	3	25	0
Lee, Manuel, Tor.†	.256	56	121	14	31	1	11	2
Lemon, Chester, Det.	.277	146	470	75	130	20	75	0
Liriano, Nelson, Tor.†	.241	37	158	29	38	2	10	13
Lombardozzi, Steve, Minn.	.238	136	432	51	103	8	38	5
Lusader, Scott, Det.*	.319	23	47	8	15	1	8	1
Lynn, Frederic, Balt.*	.253	111	396	49	100	23	60	3
Lyons, Stephen, Chi.*	.280	76	193	26	54	1	19	3
Madlock, Bill, Det.	.279	87	326	56	91	14	50	4
Manning, Richard, Mil.*	.228	97	114	21	26	0	13	4
Manrique, R. Fred, Chi.	.258	115	298	30	77	4	29	5
Martinez, Edgar, Sea.	.372	13	43	6	16	0	5	0
Marzano, John, Bos.	.244	52	168	20	41	5	24	0
Matthews, Gary, Sea.	.235	45	119	10	28	3	15	0
Mattingly, Donald, N.Y.*	.327	141	569	93	186	30	115	1

Batter and Club	AVG	G	AB	R	H	HR	RBI	SB
McDowell, Oddibe, Tex.*	.241	128	407	65	98	14	52	24
McGriff, Frederick, Tor.*	.247	107	295	58	73	20	43	3
McGwire, Mark, Oak.	.289	151	557	97	161	49	118	1
McLemore, Mark, Cal.†	.236	138	433	61	102	3	41	25
McRae, Harold, K.C.	.313	18	32	5	10	1	9	0
Meacham, Robert, N.Y.	.271	77	203	28	55	5	21	6
Miller, Darrell, Cal.	.241	53	108	14	26	4	16	1
Molitor, Paul, Mil.	.353	118	465	114	164	16	75	45
Moore, Charles, Tor.	.215	51	107	15	23	1	7	0
Morrison, James, Det.	.205	34	117	15	24	4	19	2
Moseby, Lloyd, Tor.*	.282	155	592	106	167	26	96	39
Moses, John, Sea.†	.246	116	390	58	96	3	38	23
Mulliniks, Rance, Tor.*	.310	124	332	37	103	11	44	1
Murphy, Dwayne, Oak.*	.233	82	219	39	51	8	35	4
Murray, Eddie, Balt.†	.277	160	618	89	171	30	91	1
Newman, Albert, Minn.†	.221	110	307	44	68	0	29	15
Nieto, Thomas, Minn.	.200	41	105	7	21	1	12	0
Nixon, R. Donell, Sea.	.250	46	132	17	33	3	12	21
Noboa, Milciades, Clev.	.225	39	80	7	18	0	7	1
Nokes, Matthew, Det.*	.289	135	461	69	133	32	87	2
O'Brien, Charles, Mil.	.200	10	35	2	7	0	0	0
O'Brien, Peter, Tex.*	.286	159	569	84	163	23	88	0
O'Malley, Thomas, Tex.*	.274	45	117	10	32	1	12	0
Orta, Jorge, K.C.*	.180	21	50	3	9	2	4	0
Owen, Lawrence, K.C.	.189	76	164	17	31	5	14	0
Owen, Spike, Bos.†	.259	132	437	50	113	2	48	11
Paciorek, James, Mil.	.228	48	101	16	23	2	10	1
Paciorek, Thomas, Tex.	.283	27	60	6	17	3	12	0
Pagliarulo, Mike, N.Y.*	.234	150	522	76	122	32	87	1
Parrish, Larry, Tex.	.268	152	557	79	149	32	100	3
Pasqua, Daniel, N.Y.*	.233	113	318	42	74	17	42	0
Pecota, William, K.C.	.276	66	156	22	43	3	14	5
Petralli, Eugene, Tex.†	.302	101	202	28	61	7	31	0
Pettis, Gary, Cal.†	.208	133	394	49	82	1	17	24
Phelps, Kenneth, Sea.*	.259	120	332	68	86	27	68	1
Phillips, Tony, Oak.†	.240	111	379	48	91	10	46	7
Polidor, Gustavo, Cal.	.263	63	137	12	36	2	15	0

Batter and Club	AVG	G	AB	R	H	HR	RBI	SB
Polonia, Luis, Oak.*	.287	125	435	78	125	4	49	29
Porter, Darrell, Tex.*	.238	85	130	19	31	7	21	0
Presley, James, Sea.	.247	152	575	78	142	24	88	2
Puckett, Kirby, Minn.	.332	157	624	96	207	28	99	12
Quinones, Rey, Sea.	.276	135	478	55	132	12	56	1
Quirk, James, K.C.*	.236	109	296	24	70	5	33	1
Ramos, Domingo, Sea.	.311	42	103	9	32	2	11	0
Randolph, William, N.Y.	.305	120	449	96	137	7	67	11
Ray, Johnny, Cal.†	.346	30	127	16	44	0	15	0
Rayford, Floyd, Balt.	.220	20	50	5	11	2	3	0
Redus, Gary, Chi.	.236	130	475	78	112	12	48	52
Reed, Jody, Bos.	.300	9	30	4	9	0	8	1
Reynolds, Harold, Sea.†	.275	160	530	73	146	1	35	60
Rice, James, Bos.	.277	108	404	66	112	13	62	1
Riles, Ernest, Mil.*	.261	83	276	38	72	4	38	3
Ripken, Calvin, Balt.	.252	162	624	97	157	27	98	3
Ripken, William, Balt.	.308	58	234	27	72	2	20	4
Robidoux, William, Mil.*	.194	23	62	9	12	0	4	0
Romero, Edgardo, Bos.	.272	88	235	23	64	0	14	0
Royster, Jeron, Chi.-N.Y.	.265	73	196	26	52	7	27	4
Ryal, Mark, Cal.*	.200	58	100	7	20	5	18	0
Sakata, Lenn, N.Y.	.267	19	45	5	12	2	4	0
Salas, Mark, Minn.-N.Y.*	.250	72	160	21	40	6	21	0
Salazar, Argenis, K.C.	.205	116	317	24	65	2	21	4
Schofield, Richard, Cal.	.251	134	479	52	120	9	46	19
Schroeder, Bill, Mil.	.332	75	250	35	83	14	42	5
Seitzer, Kevin, K.C.	.323	161	641	105	207	15	83	12
Sharperson, Mike, Tor.	.208	32	96	4	20	0	9	2
Sheaffer, Danny, Bos.	.121	25	66	5	8	1	5	0
Sheets, Larry, Balt.*	.316	135	469	74	148	31	94	1
Shelby, John, Balt.†	.188	21	32	4	6	1	3	0
Sheridan, Patrick, Det.*	.259	141	421	57	109	6	49	18
Sierra, Ruben, Tex.†	.263	158	643	97	169	30	109	16
Simmons, Nelson, Balt.†	.265	16	49	3	13	1	4	0
Skinner, Joel, N.Y.	.137	64	139	9	19	3	14	0
Slaught, Donald, Tex.	.224	95	237	25	53	8	16	0
Smalley, Roy, Minn.†	.275	110	309	32	85	8	34	2

Batter and Club	AVG	G	AB	R	H	HR	RBI	SB
Smith, Lonnie, K.C.	.251	48	167	26	42	3	8	9
Snyder, J. Cory, Clev.	.236	157	577	74	136	33	82	5
Stanicek, Peter, Balt.†	.274	30	113	9	31	0	9	8
Stanley, Michael, Tex.	.273	78	216	34	59	6	37	3
Steinbach, Terry, Oak.	.284	122	391	66	111	16	56	1
Sullivan, Marc, Bos.	.169	60	160	11	27	2	10	0
Surhoff, B.J., Mil.*	.299	115	395	50	118	7	68	11
Sveum, Dale, Mil.†	.252	153	535	86	135	25	95	2
Tabler, Patrick, Clev.	.307	151	553	66	170	11	86	5
Tartabull, Danilo, K.C.	.309	158	582	95	180	34	101	9
Tettleton, Mickey, Oak.†	.194	82	211	19	41	8	26	1
Thurman, Gary, K.C.	.296	27	81	12	24	0	5	7
Tolleson, J. Wayne, N.Y.†	.221	121	349	48	77	1	22	5
Trammell, Alan, Det.	.343	151	597	109	205	28	105	21
Upshaw, Willie, Tor.*	.244	150	512	68	125	15	58	10
Valle, David, Sea.	.256	95	324	40	83	12	53	2
Walewander, James, Det.†	.241	53	54	24	13	1	4	2
Walker, Gregory, Chi.*	.256	157	566	85	145	27	94	2
Ward, Gary, N.Y.	.248	146	529	65	131	16	78	9
Washington, C., N.Y.*	.279	102	312	42	87	9	44	10
Washington, Ronald, Balt.	.203	26	79	7	16	1	6	0
Whitaker, Louis, Det.*	.265	149	604	110	160	16	59	13
White, Devon, Cal.†	.263	159	639	103	168	24	87	32
White, Frank, K.C.	.245	154	563	67	138	17	78	1
Whitt, L. Ernest, Tor.*	.269	135	446	57	120	19	75	0
Wiggins, Alan, Balt.†	.232	85	306	37	71	1	15	20
Wilkerson, Curtis, Tex.†	.268	85	138	28	37	2	14	6
Williams, Edward, Clev.	.172	22	64	9	11	1	4	0
Williams, Kenneth, Chi.	.281	116	391	48	110	11	50	21
Wilson, Willie, K.C.†	.279	146	610	97	170	4	30	59
Winfield, David, N.Y.	.275	156	575	83	158	27	97	5
Wynegar, Harold, Cal.†	.207	31	92	4	19	0	5	0
Young, Michael, Balt.†	.240	110	363	46	87	16	39	10
Yount, Robin, Mil.	.312	158	635	99	198	21	103	19
Zuvella, Paul, N.Y.	.176	14	34	2	6	0	0	0

AMERICAN LEAGUE
Pitching

(80 or more innings pitched)
*Throws Left-handed

Pitcher and Club	W	L	ERA	G	IP	H	BB	SO
Alexander, Doyle, Det.	9	0	1.53	11	88.1	63	26	44
Bailes, Scott, Clev.*	7	8	4.64	39	120.1	145	47	65
Bankhead, M. Scott, Sea.	9	8	5.42	27	149.1	168	37	95
Bannister, Floyd, Chi.*	16	11	3.58	34	228.2	216	49	124
Bell, Eric, Balt.*	10	13	5.45	33	165.0	174	78	111
Berenguer, Juan, Minn....	8	1	3.94	47	112.0	100	47	110
Black, Harry, K.C.*	8	6	3.60	29	122.1	126	35	61
Blyleven, Bert, Minn.	15	12	4.01	37	267.0	249	101	196
Boddicker, Michael, Balt. ..	10	12	4.18	33	226.0	212	78	152
Bosio, Christopher, Mil. ..	11	8	5.24	46	170.0	187	50	150
Buice, DeWayne, Cal.	6	7	3.39	57	114.0	87	40	109
Candelaria, John, Cal.* ...	8	6	4.71	20	116.2	127	20	74
Candiotti, Thomas, Clev....	7	18	4.78	32	201.2	193	93	111
Carlton, S., Clev.-Minn.*	6	14	5.74	32	152.0	165	86	91
Cerutti, John, Tor.*	11	4	4.40	44	151.1	144	59	92
Clancy, James, Tor.	15	11	3.54	37	241.1	234	80	180
Clemens, W. Roger, Bos. ..	20	9	2.97	36	281.2	248	83	256
Clements, Patrick, N.Y.* ..	3	3	4.95	55	80.0	91	30	36
Crim, Charles, Mil.	6	8	3.67	53	130.0	133	39	56
DeLeon, Jose, Chi.	11	12	4.02	33	206.0	177	97	153
Dixon, Kenneth, Balt.	7	10	6.43	34	105.0	128	27	91
Dotson, Richard, Chi.	11	12	4.17	31	211.1	201	86	114
Eckersley, Dennis, Oak....	6	8	3.03	54	115.2	99	17	113
Eichhorn, Mark, Tor.	10	6	3.17	89	127.2	110	52	96
Farr, Steven, K.C.	4	3	4.15	47	91.0	97	44	88
Finley, Charles, Cal.*	2	7	4.67	35	90.2	102	43	63
Flanagan, M., Balt.-Tor.* ...	6	8	4.06	23	144.0	148	51	93
Fraser, William, Cal.	10	10	3.92	36	176.2	160	63	106
Frazier, George, Minn.	5	5	4.98	54	81.1	77	51	58
Gardner, Wesley, Bos.	3	6	5.42	49	89.2	98	42	70
Gubicza, Mark, K.C.	13	18	3.98	35	241.2	231	120	166

Pitcher and Club	W	L	ERA	G	IP	H	BB	SO
Guetterman, Lee, Sea.*	11	4	3.81	25	113.1	117	35	42
Guidry, Ronald, N.Y.*	5	8	3.67	22	117.2	111	38	96
Guzman, Jose, Tex.	14	14	4.67	37	208.1	196	82	143
Habyan, John, Balt.	6	7	4.80	27	116.1	110	40	64
Harris, Greg, Tex.	5	10	4.86	42	140.2	157	56	106
Henke, Thomas, Tor.	0	6	2.49	72	94.0	62	25	128
Henneman, Michael, Det.	11	3	2.98	55	96.2	86	30	75
Higuera, Teodoro, Mil.*	18	10	3.85	35	261.2	236	87	240
Hough, Charles, Tex.	18	13	3.79	40	285.1	238	124	223
Hudson, Charles, N.Y.	11	7	3.61	35	154.2	137	57	100
Hurst, Bruce, Bos.*	15	13	4.41	33	238.2	239	76	190
Jackson, Danny, K.C.*	9	18	4.02	36	224.0	219	109	152
John, Thomas, N.Y.*	13	6	4.03	33	187.2	212	47	63
Jones, Douglas, Clev.	6	5	3.15	49	91.1	101	24	87
Key, James, Tor.*	17	8	2.76	36	261.0	210	66	161
Kilgus, Paul, Tex.*	2	7	4.13	25	89.1	95	31	42
Langston, Mark, Sea.*	19	13	3.84	35	272.0	242	114	262
LaPoint, David, Chi.*	6	3	2.94	14	82.2	69	31	43
Lazorko, Jack, Cal.	5	6	4.59	26	117.2	108	44	55
Leibrandt, Charles, K.C.*	16	11	3.41	35	240.1	235	74	151
Long, William, Chi.	8	8	4.37	29	169.0	179	28	72
McGregor, Scott, Balt.*	2	7	6.64	26	85.1	112	35	39
Mohorcic, Dale, Tex.	7	6	2.99	74	99.1	88	19	48
Moore, Michael, Sea.	9	19	4.71	33	231.0	268	84	115
Morgan, Michael, Sea.	12	17	4.65	34	207.0	245	53	85
Morris, John, Det.	18	11	3.38	34	266.0	227	93	208
Musselman, J., Tor.*	12	5	4.15	68	89.0	75	54	54
Nelson, W. Eugene, Oak.	6	5	3.93	54	123.2	120	35	94
Niekro, J., N.Y.-Minn.	7	13	5.33	27	147.0	155	64	84
Niekro, P., Clev.-Tor.	7	13	6.10	25	135.2	157	60	64
Nieves, Juan, Mil.*	14	8	4.88	34	195.2	199	100	163
Nipper, Albert, Bos.	11	12	5.43	30	174.0	196	62	89
Nunez, Jose, Tor.	5	2	5.01	37	97.0	91	58	99
Ontiveros, Steven, Oak.	10	8	4.00	35	150.2	141	50	97
Petry, Daniel, Det.	9	7	5.61	30	134.2	148	76	93
Plunk, Eric, Oak.	4	6	4.74	32	95.0	91	62	90
Rasmussen, D., N.Y.*	9	7	4.75	26	146.0	145	55	89

Pitcher and Club	W	L	ERA	G	IP	H	BB	SO
Reardon, Jeffrey, Minn. . .	8	8	4.48	63	80.1	70	28	83
Reed, Jerry, Sea.	1	2	3.42	39	81.2	79	24	51
Reuss, Jerry, Cal.*	4	5	5.25	17	82.1	112	17	37
Rhoden, Richard, N.Y.	16	10	3.86	30	181.2	184	61	107
Righetti, David, N.Y.*	8	6	3.51	60	95.0	95	44	77
Rijo, Jose, Oak. . . . . :	2	7	5.90	21	82.1	106	41	67
Robinson, Jeff, Det.	9	6	5.37	29	127.1	132	54	98
Russell, Jeffrey, Tex.	5	4	4.44	52	97.1	109	52	56
Saberhagen, Bret, K.C. . . .	18	10	3.36	33	257.0	246	53	163
Schiraldi, Calvin, Bos.	8	5	4.41	62	83.2	75	40	93
Schmidt, David, Balt.	10	5	3.77	35	124.0	128	26	70
Schrom, Kenneth, Clev. . . .	6	13	6.50	32	153.2	185	57	61
Sellers, Jeffrey, Bos.	7	8	5.28	25	139.2	161	61	99
Smithson, Mike, Minn.	4	7	5.94	21	109.0	126	38	53
Stanley, Robert, Bos.	4	15	5.01	34	152.2	198	42	67
Stewart, David, Oak.	20	13	3.68	37	261.1	224	105	205
Stieb, David, Tor.	13	9	4.09	33	185.0	164	87	115
Stoddard, Timothy, N.Y. . .	4	3	3.50	57	92.2	83	30	78
Straker, Lester, Minn.	8	10	4.37	31	154.1	150	59	76
Sutton, Donald, Cal.	11	11	4.70	35	191.2	199	41	99
Swindell, Greg, Clev.*	3	8	5.10	16	102.1	112	37	97
Tanana, Frank, Det.*	15	10	3.91	34	218.2	216	56	146
Terrell, C. Walter, Det. . . .	17	10	4.05	35	244.2	254	94	143
Thigpen, Robert, Chi.	7	5	2.73	51	89.0	86	24	52
Viola, Frank, Minn.*	17	10	2.90	36	251.2	230	66	197
Wegman, William, Mil. . . .	12	11	4.24	34	225.0	229	53	102
Williams, M., Tex.*	8	6	3.23	85	108.2	63	94	129
Williamson, Mark, Balt. . .	8	9	4.03	61	125.0	122	41	73
Winn, James, Chi.	4	6	4.79	56	94.0	95	62	44
Witt, Michael, Cal.	16	14	4.01	36	247.0	252	84	192
Witt, Robert, Tex.	8	10	4.91	26	143.0	114	140	160
Yett, Richard, Clev.	3	9	5.25	37	97.2	96	49	59
Young, Curtis, Oak.*	13	7	4.08	31	203.0	194	44	124

NATIONAL LEAGUE
Batting
(42 or more at-bats)
*Bats Left-handed   †Switch-Hitter

Batter and Club	AVG	G	AB	R	H	HR	RBI	SB
Abner, Shawn, S.D.	.277	16	47	5	13	2	7	1
Aguayo, Luis, Phil.	.206	94	209	25	43	12	21	0
Aldrete, Michael, S.F.*	.325	126	357	50	116	9	51	6
Almon, William, Pitt.-N.Y.	.230	68	74	13	17	0	5	1
Anderson, David, L.A.	.234	108	265	32	62	1	13	9
Ashby, Alan, Hou.†	.288	125	386	53	111	14	63	0
Backman, Walter, N.Y.†	.250	94	300	43	75	1	23	11
Bailey, J. Mark, Hou.†	.203	35	64	5	13	0	3	1
Bass, Kevin, Hou.†	.284	157	592	83	168	19	85	21
Bell, David, Cin.	.284	143	522	74	148	17	70	4
Belliard, Rafael, Pitt.	.207	81	203	26	42	1	15	5
Benedict, Bruce, Atl.	.147	37	95	4	14	1	5	0
Berra, Dale, Hou.	.178	19	45	3	8	0	2	0
Bielecki, Michael, Pitt.	.063	8	16	0	1	0	0	0
Blauser, Jeffrey, Alt.	.242	51	165	11	40	2	15	7
Bochy, Bruce, S.D.	.160	38	75	8	12	2	11	0
Bonds, Barry, Pitt.*	.261	150	551	99	144	25	59	32
Bonilla, Roberto, Pitt.†	.300	141	466	58	140	15	77	3
Booker, Roderick, St.L.*	.277	44	47	9	13	0	8	2
Bream, Sidney, Pitt.*	.275	149	516	64	142	13	65	9
Brenly, Robert, S.F.	.267	123	375	55	100	18	51	10
Brooks, Hubert, Mtl.	.263	112	430	57	113	14	72	4
Brown, Chris, S.F.-S.D.	.237	82	287	34	68	12	40	4
Browning, Thomas, Cin.*	.154	34	52	2	8	0	6	1
Brumley, Mike, Chi.†	.202	39	104	8	21	1	9	7
Bryant, Ralph, L.A.*	.246	46	69	7	17	2	10	2
Caminiti, Kenneth, Hou.†	.246	63	203	10	50	3	23	0
Candaele, Casey, Mtl.†	.272	138	449	62	122	1	23	7
Cangelosi, John, Pitt.†	.275	104	182	44	50	4	18	21
Carman, Donald, Phil.*	.082	35	61	2	5	0	4	0
Carter, Gary, N.Y.	.235	139	523	55	123	20	83	0

Batter and Club	AVG	G	AB	R	H	HR	RBI	SB
Clark, Jack, St.L.	.286	131	419	93	120	35	106	1
Clark, William, S.F.*	.308	150	529	89	163	35	91	5
Coleman, Vincent, St.L.†...	.289	151	623	121	180	3	43	109
Coles, Darnell, Pitt.	.227	40	119	20	27	6	24	1
Collins, David, Cin.†	.294	57	85	19	25	0	5	9
Concepcion, David, Cin. ...	.319	104	279	32	89	1	33	4
Cora, Jose, S.D.†	.237	77	241	23	57	0	13	15
Cox, Danny, St.L.	.116	32	69	3	8	0	1	0
Cruz, Jose, Hou.*	.241	126	365	47	88	11	38	4
Daniels, Kalvoski, Cin.* ...	.334	108	368	73	123	26	64	26
Darling, Ronald, N.Y.	.123	32	65	5	8	0	4	0
Darwin, Danny, Hou.	.182	35	66	2	12	0	4	1
Daulton, Darren, Phil.*	.194	53	129	10	25	3	13	0
Davis, Charles, S.F.†	.250	149	500	80	125	24	76	16
Davis, Eric, Cin.	.293	129	474	120	139	37	100	50
Davis, Glenn, Hou.	.251	151	578	70	145	27	93	4
Davis, Jody, Chi.............	.248	125	428	57	106	19	51	1
Dawson, Andre, Chi.	.287	153	621	90	178	49	137	11
Dayett, Brian, Chi...........	.277	97	177	20	49	5	25	0
Dernier, Robert, Chi........	.317	93	199	38	63	8	21	16
Deshaies, James, Hou.* ...	.094	26	53	2	5	0	3	0
Devereaux, Michael, L.A.	.222	19	54	7	12	0	4	3
Diaz, Baudilio, Cin.	.270	140	496	49	134	15	82	1
Diaz, Michael, Pitt..........	.241	103	241	28	58	16	48	1
Doran, William, Hou.†	.283	162	625	82	177	16	79	31
Downs, Kelly, S.F............	.143	41	56	1	8	0	6	0
Drabek, Douglas, Pitt.	.119	30	59	2	7	0	4	0
Dravecky, David, S.D.-S.F.	.143	49	56	3	8	0	0	1
Driessen, Daniel, St.L.* ...	.233	24	60	5	14	1	11	0
Duncan, Mariano, L.A.†...	.215	76	261	31	56	6	18	11
Dunne, Michael, Pitt.	.094	23	53	2	5	0	3	0
Dunston, Shawon, Chi.	.246	95	346	40	85	5	22	12
Durham, Leon, Chi.*	.273	131	439	70	120	27	63	2
Dykstra, Leonard, N.Y.* ...	.285	132	431	86	123	10	43	27
Easler, Michael, Phil.*	.282	33	110	7	31	1	10	0
Engle, R. David, Mtl.........	.226	59	84	7	19	1	14	1
Esasky, Nicholas, Cin.	.272	100	346	48	94	22	59	0

Batter and Club	AVG	G	AB	R	H	HR	RBI	SB
Fermin, Felix, Pitt.	.250	23	68	6	17	0	4	0
Fernandez, Sid, N.Y.*	.163	29	43	2	7	0	2	0
Fisher, Brian, Pitt.	.190	37	58	6	11	2	9	0
Fitzgerald, Michael, Mtl.	.240	107	287	32	69	3	36	3
Flannery, Timothy, S.D.* ...	.228	106	276	23	63	0	20	2
Foley, Thomas, Mtl.*........	.293	106	280	35	82	5	28	6
Ford, Curtis, St.L.*	.285	89	228	32	65	3	26	11
Forsch, Robert, St.L.	.298	34	57	9	17	2	8	0
Francona, Terry, Cin.*	.227	102	207	16	47	3	12	2
Galarraga, Andres, Mtl.	.305	147	551	72	168	13	90	7
Gant, Ronald, Atl.	.265	21	83	9	22	2	9	4
Garner, Philip, Hou.-L.A. ...	.206	113	238	29	49	5	23	6
Garvey, Steven, S.D.	.211	27	76	5	16	1	9	0
Gooden, Dwight, N.Y........	.219	25	64	4	14	0	4	0
Grant, Mark, S.F.-S.D.	.091	34	44	1	4	0	1	0
Griffey, G. Kenneth, Atl.* ...	.286	122	399	65	114	14	64	4
Gross, Gregory, Phil.*	.286	114	133	14	38	1	12	0
Gross, Kevin, Phil...........	.190	34	63	4	12	1	4	0
Guerrero, Pedro, L.A........	.338	152	545	89	184	27	89	9
Gullickson, William, Cin. ...	.208	27	53	4	11	1	3	0
Gwynn, Anthony, S.D.*	.370	157	589	119	218	7	54	56
Hall, Albert, Atl.†	.284	92	292	54	83	3	24	33
Hamilton, Jeffrey, L.A.......	.217	35	83	5	18	0	1	0
Hammaker, Atlee, S.F.†	.123	31	57	0	7	0	3	0
Harper, Terry, Pitt...........	.288	36	66	8	19	1	7	0
Hatcher, Michael, L.A.	.282	101	287	27	81	7	42	2
Hatcher, William, Hou.......	.296	141	564	96	167	11	63	53
Hayes, Von, Phil.*	.277	158	556	84	154	21	84	16
Heaton, Neal, Mtl.*..........	.209	32	67	6	14	0	6	1
Heep, Daniel, L.A.*	.163	60	98	7	16	0	9	1
Hernandez, Keith, N.Y.*	.290	154	587	87	170	18	89	0
Herr, Thomas, St.L.†	.263	141	510	73	134	2	83	19
Hershiser, Orel, L.A.	.211	40	90	10	19	0	7	2
Hoffman, Glenn, L.A.	.220	40	132	10	29	0	10	0
Hoffman, Guy, Cin.*	.111	36	45	2	5	0	5	0
Hubbard, Glenn, Atl.	.264	141	443	69	117	5	38	1
Hughes, Keith, Phil.*	.263	37	76	8	20	0	10	0

Batter and Club	AVG	G	AB	R	H	HR	RBI	SB
Jackson, Charles, Hou.	.211	35	71	3	15	1	6	1
James, Dion, Atl.*	.312	134	494	80	154	10	61	10
James, D. Chris., Phil.	.293	115	358	48	105	17	54	3
Jefferson, Stanley, S.D.† ...	.230	116	422	59	97	8	29	34
Jeltz, L. Steven, Phil.†	.232	114	293	37	68	0	12	1
Johnson, Howard, N.Y.†	.265	157	554	93	147	36	99	32
Johnson, K. Lance, St.L.*	.220	33	59	4	13	0	7	6
Johnson, Wallace, Mtl.†	.247	75	85	7	21	1	14	5
Jones, James, S.D.	.163	32	49	7	8	1	3	0
Jones, Tracy, Cin.	.290	117	359	53	104	10	44	31
Knepper, Robert, Hou.*	.098	33	51	2	5	0	1	0
Kruk, John, S.D.*	.313	138	447	72	140	20	91	18
Krukow, Michael, S.F.	.167	30	54	1	9	0	7	0
LaCoss, Michael, S.F.	.060	39	50	2	3	0	3	0
Lake, Steven, St.L.	.251	74	179	19	45	2	19	0
Lancaster, Lester, Chi.	.082	27	49	2	4	0	2	0
Landreaux, Ken, L.A.*	.203	115	182	17	37	6	23	5
Landrum, Terry, St.L.-L.A.	.222	81	117	13	26	1	10	2
Larkin, Barry, Cin.	.244	125	439	64	107	12	43	21
LaValliere, Michael, Pitt.*	.300	121	340	33	102	1	36	0
Law, Vance, Mtl.	.273	133	436	52	119	12	56	8
Leonard, Jeffrey, S.F.	.280	131	503	70	141	19	63	16
Lind, Jose, Pitt.	.322	35	143	21	46	0	11	2
Lindeman, James, St.L.	.208	75	207	20	43	8	28	3
Lopes, David, Hou.	.233	47	43	4	10	1	6	2
Lyons, Barry, N.Y.	.254	53	130	15	33	4	24	0
Mack, Shane, S.D.	.239	105	238	28	57	4	25	4
Maddux, Gregory, Chi.	.119	34	42	3	5	0	2	0
Madlock, Bill, L.A.	.180	21	61	5	11	3	7	0
Magadan, David, N.Y.*	.318	85	192	21	61	3	24	0
Magrane, Joseph, St.L.	.135	28	52	5	7	1	3	0
Mahler, Richard, Atl.	.169	40	65	4	11	0	5	0
Maldonado, Candido, S.F.	.292	118	442	69	129	20	85	8
Marshall, Michael, L.A.	.294	104	402	45	118	16	72	0
Martinez, Carmelo, S.D.	.273	139	447	59	122	15	70	5
Martinez, David, Chi.*	.292	142	459	70	134	8	36	16
Martinez, J. Dennis, Mtl....	.065	22	46	5	3	0	3	0

Batter and Club	AVG	G	AB	R	H	HR	RBI	SB
Mathews, Gregory, St.L. ...	.191	32	68	5	13	0	3	0
Matthews, Gary, Chi.	.262	44	42	3	11	0	8	0
Mazzilli, Lee, N.Y.†	.306	88	124	26	38	3	24	5
McClendon, Lloyd, Cin.	.208	45	72	8	15	2	13	1
McGee, Willie, St.L.†	.285	153	620	76	177	11	105	16
McGriff, Terence, Cin........	.225	34	89	6	20	2	11	0
McReynolds, Kevin, N.Y.....	.276	151	590	86	163	29	95	14
Melvin, Robert, S.F.	.199	84	246	31	49	11	31	0
Miller, Keith, N.Y.	.373	25	51	14	19	0	1	8
Milner, Eddie, S.F.*	.252	101	214	38	54	4	19	10
Mitchell, Kevin, S.D.-S.F. ...	.280	131	464	68	130	22	70	9
Moreland, B. Keith, Chi.	.266	153	563	63	150	27	88	3
Morris, John, St.L.*	.261	101	157	22	41	3	23	5
Morrison, James, Pitt......	.264	96	348	41	92	9	46	8
Moyer, Jamie, Chi.*	.230	39	61	3	14	0	3	0
Mumphrey, Jerry, Chi.†.....	.333	118	309	41	103	13	44	1
Murphy, Dale, Atl.	.295	159	566	115	167	44	105	16
Nettles, Graig, Atl.*	.209	112	177	16	37	5	33	1
Nichols, T. Reid, Mtl........	.265	77	147	22	39	4	20	2
Noce, Paul, Chi.	.228	70	180	17	41	3	14	5
Oberkfell, Kenneth, Atl.*....	.280	135	508	59	142	3	48	3
Oester, Ronald, Cin.†	.253	69	237	28	60	2	23	2
O'Neill, Paul, Cin.*	.256	84	160	24	41	7	28	2
Oquendo, Jose, St.L.†.....	.286	116	248	43	71	1	24	4
Ortiz, Adalberto, Pitt.	.271	75	192	16	52	1	22	0
Pagnozzi, Thomas, St.L. ...	.188	27	48	8	9	2	9	1
Palmeiro, Rafael, Chi.*	.276	84	221	32	61	14	30	2
Palmer, David, Atl...........	.125	28	48	4	6	1	5	0
Pankovits, James, Hou.	.230	50	61	7	14	1	8	2
Parker, David, Cin.*	.253	153	589	77	149	26	97	7
Parrish, Lance, Phil.	.245	130	466	42	114	17	67	0
Pedrique, A., N.Y.-Pitt.	.294	93	252	24	74	1	27	5
Pena, Adalberto, Hou.	.152	21	46	5	7	0	0	0
Pena, Antonio, St.L.	.214	116	384	40	82	5	44	6
Pendleton, Terry, St.L.†	.286	159	583	82	167	12	96	19
Perry, Gerald, Atl.*	.270	142	533	77	144	12	74	42
Power, Ted, Cin.	.119	35	59	3	7	1	4	0

Batter and Club	AVG	G	AB	R	H	HR	RBI	SB
Puhl, Terrance, Hou.*	.230	90	122	9	28	2	15	1
Quinones, Luis, Chi.†	.218	49	101	12	22	0	8	0
Raines, Timothy, Mtl.†	.330	139	530	123	175	18	68	50
Ramirez, Rafael, Atl.	.263	56	179	22	47	1	21	6
Ramsey, Michael, L.A.†	.232	48	125	18	29	0	12	2
Rawley, Shane, Phil.	.152	37	79	5	12	0	4	1
Ray, Johnny, Pitt.†	.273	123	472	48	129	5	54	4
Ready, Randy, S.D.	.309	124	350	69	108	12	54	7
Reed, Jeffrey, Mtl.*	.213	75	207	15	44	1	21	0
Reuschel, R., Pitt.-S.F.	.139	34	79	8	11	1	10	1
Reynolds, G. Craig, Hou.*	.254	135	374	35	95	4	28	5
Reynolds, R. J., Pitt.†	.260	117	335	47	87	7	51	14
Reynolds, Ronn, Hou.	.167	38	102	5	17	1	7	0
Roenicke, Gary, Atl.	.219	67	151	25	33	9	28	0
Roenicke, Ronald, Phil.†	.167	63	78	9	13	1	4	1
Ruffin, Bruce, Phil.	.055	35	73	3	4	0	3	0
Runge, Paul, Atl.	.213	27	47	9	10	3	8	0
Russell, John, Phil.	.145	24	62	5	9	3	8	0
Ryan, L. Nolan, Hou.	.062	34	65	2	4	1	4	0
Salazar, Luis, S.D.	.254	84	189	13	48	3	17	3
Samuel, Juan, Phil.	.272	160	655	113	178	28	100	35
Sandberg, Ryne, Chi.	.294	132	523	81	154	16	59	21
Santana, Rafael, N.Y.	.255	139	439	41	112	5	44	1
Santiago, Benito, S.D.	.300	146	546	64	164	18	79	21
Sax, Stephen, L.A.	.280	157	610	84	171	6	46	37
Schmidt, Michael, Phil.	.293	147	522	88	153	35	113	2
Schu, Richard, Phil.	.235	92	196	24	46	7	23	0
Scioscia, Michael, L.A.*	.265	142	461	44	122	6	38	7
Scott, Michael, Hou.	.125	36	80	4	10	0	3	0
Sebra, Robert, Mtl.	.157	36	51	2	8	0	1	0
Shelby, John, L.A.†	.277	120	476	61	132	21	69	16
Show, Eric, S.D.	.071	34	70	5	5	0	2	0
Simmons, Ted, Atl.†	.277	73	177	20	49	4	30	1
Smith, Bryn, Mtl.	.136	26	44	2	6	0	4	0
Smith, Osborne, St.L.†	.303	158	600	104	182	0	75	43
Smith, Zane, Atl.*	.132	41	76	6	10	0	6	1
Speier, Chris, S.F.	.249	111	317	39	79	11	39	4

Batter and Club	AVG	G	AB	R	H	HR	RBI	SB
Spilman, W. Harry, S.F.*	.267	83	90	5	24	1	14	1
Steels, James, S.D.*	.191	62	68	9	13	0	6	3
Stefero, John, Mtl.*	.196	18	56	4	11	1	3	0
Stillwell, Kurt, Cin.†	.258	131	395	54	102	4	33	4
Stone, Jeffrey, Phil.*	.256	66	125	19	32	1	16	3
Strawberry, Darryl, N.Y.*	.284	154	532	108	151	39	104	36
Stubbs, Franklin, L.A.*	.233	129	386	48	90	16	52	8
Sundberg, James, Chi.	.201	61	139	9	28	4	15	0
Sutcliffe, Richard, Chi.*	.148	35	81	8	12	0	6	1
Templeton, Garry, S.D.†	.222	148	510	42	113	5	48	14
Teufel, Timothy, N.Y.	.308	97	299	55	92	14	61	3
Thomas, Andres, Atl.	.231	82	324	29	75	5	39	6
Thompson, Milton, Phil.*	.302	150	527	86	159	7	43	46
Thompson, Robert, S.F.	.262	132	420	62	110	10	44	16
Thon, Richard, Hou.	.212	32	66	6	14	1	3	3
Treadway, Jeff, Cin.*	.333	23	84	9	28	2	4	1
Trevino, Alejandro, L.A.	.222	72	144	16	32	3	16	1
Trillo, J. Manuel, Chi.	.294	108	214	27	63	8	26	0
Uribe, Jose, S.F.†	.291	95	309	44	90	5	30	12
Valenzuela, F., L.A.*	.141	38	92	4	13	1	8	0
Van Slyke, Andrew, Pitt.*	.293	157	564	93	165	21	82	34
Virgil, Osvaldo, Atl.	.247	123	429	57	106	27	72	0
Walker, Cleotha, Chi.†	.200	47	105	15	21	0	7	11
Wallach, Timothy, Mtl.	.298	153	593	89	177	26	123	9
Walling, Dennis, Hou.*	.283	110	325	45	92	5	33	5
Wasinger, Mark, S.F.	.275	44	80	16	22	1	3	2
Webster, Mitchell, Mtl.†	.281	156	588	101	165	15	63	33
Welch, Robert, L.A.	.157	38	83	5	13	0	5	0
Whitson, Eddie, S.D.	.123	36	65	1	8	0	4	0
Williams, Matthew, S.F.	.188	84	245	28	46	8	21	4
Wilson, Glenn, Phil.	.264	154	569	55	150	14	54	3
Wilson, William, N.Y.†	.299	124	385	58	115	9	34	21
Winingham, H., Mtl.*	.239	137	347	34	83	4	41	29
Woodson, Tracy, L.A.	.228	53	136	14	31	1	11	1
Wynne, Marvell, S.D.*	.250	98	188	17	47	2	24	11
Young, Gerald, Hou.†	.321	71	274	44	88	1	15	26
Youngblood, Joel, S.F.	.253	69	91	9	23	3	11	1

NATIONAL LEAGUE
Pitching
(40 or more innings pitched)
*Throws Left-handed

Pitcher and Club	W	L	ERA	G	IP	H	BB	SO
Acker, James, Atl.	4	9	4.16	68	114.2	109	51	68
Aguilera, Richard, N.Y. ..11		3	3.60	18	115.0	124	33	77
Alexander, Doyle, Atl.	5	10	4.13	16	117.2	115	27	64
Andersen, Larry, Hou.	9	5	3.45	67	101.2	95	41	94
Assenmacher, Paul, Atl.* ..	1	1	5.10	52	54.2	58	24	39
Bedrosian, Stephen, Phil.	5	3	2.83	65	89.0	79	28	74
Bielecki, Michael, Pitt.....	2	3	4.73	8	45.2	43	12	25
Booker, Gregory, S.D.	1	1	3.16	44	68.1	62	30	17
Browning, Thomas, Cin.* 10		13	5.02	32	183.0	201	61	117
Burke, Timothy, Mtl.	7	0	1.19	55	91.0	64	17	58
Calhoun, Jeffrey, Phil.* ...	3	1	1.48	42	42.2	25	26	31
Carman, Donald, Phil.* ...13		11	4.22	35	211.0	194	69	125
Childress, Rodney, Hou...	1	2	2.98	32	48.1	46	18	26
Comstock, K., S.F.-S.D.* ..	2	1	4.61	41	56.2	52	31	59
Cone, David, N.Y.	5	6	3.71	21	99.1	87	44	68
Conroy, Timothy, St.L.* ..	3	2	5.53	10	40.2	48	25	22
Cox, Danny, St.L. 11		9	3.88	31	199.1	224	71	101
Darling, Ronald, N.Y.......12		8	4.29	32	207.2	183	96	167
Darwin, Danny, Hou.......	9	10	3.59	33	195.2	184	69	134
Davis, George, S.D.	2	7	6.18	21	62.2	70	36	37
Davis, Mark, S.F.-S.D.* ...	9	8	3.99	63	133.0	123	59	98
Dawley, William, St.L.	5	8	4.47	60	96.2	93	38	65
Dayley, Kenneth, St.L.*...	9	5	2.66	53	61.0	52	33	63
Dedmon, Jeffrey, Atl.	3	4	3.91	53	89.2	82	42	40
Deshaies, James, Hou.*..11		6	4.62	26	152.0	149	57	104
DiPino, Frank, Chi.*.......	3	3	3.15	69	80.0	75	34	61
Downs, Kelly, S.F..........12		9	3.63	41	186.0	185	67	137
Drabek, Douglas, Pitt. 11		12	3.88	29	176.1	165	46	120
Dravecky, D., S.D.-S.F.* ..10		12	3.43	48	191.1	186	64	138
Dunne, Michael, Pitt. 13		6	3.03	23	163.1	143	68	72
Fernandez, Sid., N.Y.* 12		8	3.81	28	156.0	130	67	134

Pitcher and Club	W	L	ERA	G	IP	H	BB	SO
Fisher, Brian, Pitt.	11	9	4.52	37	185.1	185	72	117
Forsch, Robert, St.L.	11	7	4.32	33	179.0	189	45	89
Franco, John, Cin.*	8	5	2.52	68	82.0	76	27	61
Garber, H. Eugene, Atl.	8	10	4.41	49	69.1	87	28	48
Garrelts, Scott, S.F.	11	7	3.22	64	106.1	70	55	127
Glavine, Thomas, Atl.*	2	4	5.54	9	50.1	55	33	20
Gooden, Dwight, N.Y.	15	7	3.21	25	179.2	162	53	148
Gossage, Richard, S.D.	5	4	3.12	40	52.0	47	19	44
Gott, James, S.F.-Pitt.	1	2	3.41	55	87.0	81	40	90
Grant, Mark, S.F.-S.D.	7	9	4.24	33	163.1	170	73	90
Gross, Kevin, Phil.	9	16	4.35	34	200.2	205	87	110
Gullickson, William, Cin.	10	11	4.85	27	165.0	172	39	89
Hammaker, C. Atlee, S.F.*	10	10	3.58	31	168.1	159	57	107
Hawkins, M. Andy, S.D.	3	10	5.05	24	117.2	131	49	51
Heathcock, Jeff, Hou.	4	2	3.16	19	42.2	44	9	15
Heaton, Neal, Mtl.*	13	10	4.52	32	193.1	207	37	105
Hershiser, Orel, L.A.	16	16	3.06	37	264.2	247	74	190
Hillegas, Shawn, L.A.	4	3	3.57	12	58.0	52	31	51
Hoffman, Guy, Cin.*	9	10	4.37	36	158.2	160	49	87
Holton, Brian, L.A.	3	2	3.89	53	83.1	87	32	58
Honeycutt, Fred, L.A.*	2	12	4.59	27	115.2	133	45	92
Horton, Ricky, St.L.*	8	3	3.82	67	125.0	127	42	55
Howell, Kenneth, L.A.	3	4	4.91	40	55.0	54	29	60
Hume, T., Phil.-Cin.	2	4	5.36	49	84.0	89	43	33
Jackson, Michael, Phil.	3	10	4.20	55	109.1	88	56	93
Jones, Barry, Pitt.	2	4	5.61	32	43.1	55	23	28
Jones, James, S.D.	9	7	4.14	30	145.2	154	54	51
Kipper, Robert, Pitt.*	5	9	5.94	24	110.2	117	52	83
Knepper, Robert, Hou.*	8	17	5.27	33	177.2	226	54	76
Krukow, Michael, S.F.	5	6	4.80	30	163.0	182	46	104
LaCoss, Michael, S.F.	13	10	3.68	39	171.0	184	63	79
Lancaster, Lester, Chi.	8	3	4.90	27	132.1	138	51	78
Landrum, William, Cin.	3	2	4.71	44	65.0	68	34	42
Leach, Terry, N.Y.	11	1	3.22	44	131.1	132	29	61
Leary, Timothy, L.A.	3	11	4.76	39	107.2	121	36	61
Lefferts, Craig, S.D.-S.F.*	5	5	3.83	77	98.2	92	33	57
Lynch, Edward, Chi.	2	9	5.38	58	110.1	130	48	80

Pitcher and Club	W	L	ERA	G	IP	H	BB	SO
Maddux, Gregory, Chi.....	6	14	5.61	30	155.2	181	74	101
Magrane, Joseph, St.L.* ..	9	7	3.54	27	170.1	157	60	101
Mahler, Richard, Atl.	8	13	4.98	39	197.0	212	85	95
Martinez, J. Dennis, Mtl.	11	4	3.30	22	144.2	133	40	84
Mathews, Gregory, St.L.*	11	11	3.73	32	197.2	184	71	108
McClure, Robert, Mtl.* ...	6	1	3.44	52	52.1	47	20	33
McCullers, Lance, S.D. ...	8	10	3.72	78	123.1	115	59	126
McDowell, Roger, N.Y.	7	5	4.16	56	88.2	95	28	32
McGaffigan, Andrew, Mtl.	5	2	2.39	69	120.1	105	42	100
Meads, David, Hou.*......	5	3	5.55	45	48.2	60	16	32
Mitchell, John, N.Y.	3	6	4.11	20	111.2	124	36	57
Moyer, Jamie, Chi.*	12	15	5.10	35	201.0	210	97	147
Murphy, Robert, Cin.*	8	5	3.04	87	100.2	91	32	99
Myers, Randall, N.Y.*	3	6	3.96	54	75.0	61	30	92
Noles, Dickie, Chi..........	4	2	3.50	41	64.1	59	27	33
Nolte, Eric, S.D.*	2	6	3.21	12	67.1	57	36	44
Ojeda, Robert, N.Y.*	3	5	3.88	10	46.1	45	10	21
O'Neal Randall, Atl.-St.L.	4	2	5.32	17	66.0	81	26	37
Orosco, Jesse, N.Y.*	3	9	4.44	58	77.0	78	31	78
Pacillo, Patrick, Cin.	3	3	6.13	12	39.2	41	19	23
Palmer, David, Atl..........	8	11	4.90	28	152.1	169	64	111
Parrett, Jeffrey, Mtl.	7	6	4.21	45	62.0	53	30	56
Patterson, Robert, Pitt.*	1	4	6.70	15	43.0	49	22	27
Pena, Alejandro, L.A.	2	7	3.50	37	87.1	82	37	76
Perez, Pascual, Mtl........	7	0	2.30	10	70.1	52	16	58
Perry, W.P., St.L.-Cin.* ...	5	2	3.56	57	81.0	60	25	39
Power, Ted, Cin.	10	13	4.50	34	204.0	213	71	133
Puleo, Charles, Atl.........	6	8	4.23	35	123.1	122	40	99
Rasmussen, D., Cin.*.....	4	1	3.97	7	45.1	39	12	39
Rawley, Shane, Phil.*	17	11	4.39	36	229.2	250	86	123
Reuschel, R., Pitt.-S.F. ...	13	9	3.09	34	227.0	207	42	107
Ritchie, Wallace, Phil.* ...	3	2	3.75	49	6.21	60	29	45
Robinson, Don, Pitt.-S.F.	11	7	3.42	67	108.0	105	40	79
Robinson, Jeff, S.F.-Pitt.	8	9	2.85	81	123.1	89	54	101
Robinson, Ronald, Cin. ...	7	5	3.68	48	154.0	148	43	99
Ruffin, Bruce, Phil.*	11	14	4.35	35	204.2	236	73	93
Ryan, L. Nolan, Hou.	8	16	2.76	34	211.2	154	87	270

Pitcher and Club	W	L	ERA	G	IP	H	BB	SO
Sanderson, Scott, Chi. ...	8	9	4.29	32	144.2	156	50	106
Schatzeder, Daniel, Phil.*	3	1	4.06	26	37.2	40	14	28
Scott, Michael, Hou.	16	13	3.23	36	247.2	199	79	233
Sebra, Robert, Mtl.	6	15	4.42	36	177.1	184	67	156
Show, Eric, S.D.	8	16	3.84	34	206.1	188	85	117
Sisk, Douglas, N.Y.........	3	1	3.46	55	78.0	83	22	37
Smiley, John, Pitt.*	5	5	5.76	63	75.0	69	50	58
Smith, Bryn, Mtl...........	10	9	4.37	26	150.1	164	31	94
Smith, David, Hou....:.....	2	3	1.65	50	60.0	39	21	73
Smith, Lee, Chi.	4	10	3.12	62	83.2	84	32	96
Smith, Zane, Atl.*	15	10	4.09	36	242.0	245	91	130
Sorensen, Lary, Mtl.	3	4	4.72	23	47.2	56	12	21
St. Claire, Randy, Mtl.	3	3	4.03	44	67.0	64	20	43
Sutcliffe, Richard, Chi......	18	10	3.68	34	237.1	223	106	174
Taylor, Donald, Pitt.	2	3	5.74	14	53.1	48	28	37
Tekulve, Kenton, Phil.	6	4	3.09	90	105.0	96	29	60
Tibbs, Jay, Mtl.	4	5	4.99	19	83.0	95	34	54
Trout, Steven, Chi.*	6	3	3.00	11	75.0	72	27	32
Tudor, John, St.L.*	10	2	3.84	16	96.0	100	32	54
Tunnell, B. Lee, St.L.	4	4	4.84	32	74.1	90	34	49
Valenzuela, F., L.A.*	14	14	3.98	34	251.0	254	124	190
Walk, Robert, Pitt.	8	2	3.31	39	117.0	107	51	78
Welch, Robert, L.A.........	15	9	3.22	35	251.2	204	86	196
Whitson, Eddie, S.D.	10	13	4.73	36	205.2	197	64	135
Williams, Frank, Cin.......	4	0	2.30	85	105.2	101	39	60
Worrell, Todd, St.L.	8	6	2.66	75	94.2	86	34	92
Youmans, Floyd, Mtl.	9	8	4.64	23	116.1	112	47	94
Young, Matthew, L.A.* ...	5	8	4.47	47	54.1	62	17	42

BRUCE WEBER PICKS
HOW THEY'LL FINISH IN 1988

American League East

1. Milwaukee
2. Toronto
3. Detroit
4. New York
5. Boston
6. Cleveland
7. Baltimore

American League West

1. Oakland
2. Kansas City
3. Minnesota
4. Texas
5. Seattle
6. California
7. Chicago

National League East

1. New York
2. Montreal
3. St. Louis
4. Philadelphia
5. Pittsburgh
6. Chicago

National League West

1. Houston
2. San Francisco
3. Cincinnati
4. San Diego
5. Los Angeles
6. Atlanta

American League Champions: Milwaukee Brewers
National League Champions: New York Mets
World Champions: New York Mets

YOU PICK
HOW THEY'LL FINISH IN 1988

**American League
East**

1.

2.

3.

4.

5.

6.

7.

**American League
West**

1.

2.

3.

4.

5.

6.

7.

**National League
East**

1.

2.

3.

4.

5.

6.

**National League
West**

1.

2.

3.

4.

5.

6.

American League Champions:

National League Champions:

World Champions: